novum pro

IAN LOVELL

WAYWARD JAMES

novum pro

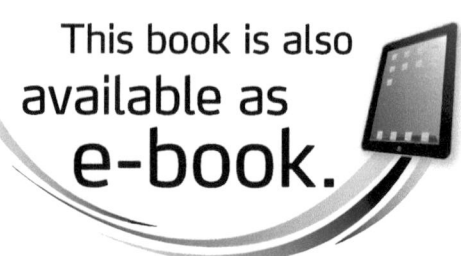

www.novum-publishing.co.uk

© 2023 novum publishing

ISBN 978-3-99146-017-6
Editing: Charlotte Middleton
Cover photos: Vbaleha, Aleksandr Kondratov I Dreamstime.com
Cover design, layout & typesetting: novum publishing

All rights of distribution, including via film, radio, and television, photomechanical reproduction, audio storage media, electronic data storage media, and the reprinting of portions of text, are reserved.

www.novum-publishing.co.uk

Printed in the European Union on environmentally friendly, chlorine- and acid-free paper.

*Those dark, stark feelings etched into the mind,
for him would seem to offer no escape.*

*He tried his best to cling onto sanity,
but still they would eat away at every thought of light.*

Welcome to the world of Jim Staley.

Contents

Chapter 1 9
Chapter 2 13
Chapter 3 20
Chapter 4 26
Chapter 5 31
Chapter 6 37
Chapter 7 41
Chapter 8 46
Chapter 9 56
Chapter 10 62
Chapter 11 71
Chapter 12 77
Chapter 13 83
Chapter 14 91
Chapter 15 97
Chapter 16 107

Chapter 17	110
Chapter 18	114
Chapter 19	115
Chapter 20	118
Chapter 21	124
Chapter 22	128
Chapter 23	133
Chapter 24	136
Chapter 25	140
Chapter 26	147
Chapter 27	152
Chapter 28	156
Chapter 29	163
Chapter 30	168
Chapter 31	171
Chapter 32	173
Ben's song	179

Chapter 1

Looking back, those school days were dull with day-to-day unacceptance by all. Well, that's the way Jim and his friends felt about it. He had a passion for annoying the other kids and teachers alike; it was the only thing that got him through each day.

When he was there, that is.

School never really agreed with him. He would often drift off in class, away from the monotonous noise cascading from his teacher's mouth. The words floated out over his head, through the window into those grey english East Midlands skies along with his mind. He longed to be out of that place, and when that day came, it was the best he had felt for a long time.

Jim always felt he had issues with his state of mind, brought to the forefront by his erratic and unpredictable behaviour, which would arise more often than not through those school days, but they continued to plague him. There was nothing he could pinpoint (apart from school, that is) that triggered these issues. He always thought he could handle them.

His friends always looked out for him, as he would often slide to another place that challenged his wellbeing. This was not helped by the considerable amounts of drugs (weed/cannabis) for now, plus the alcohol that he would consume.

He always stated that it levelled him out and took him away from any normality, but in reality his mind was spinning more from this self-medication. But still they were always concerned with his wellbeing, even if it didn't show, because they were always there, right beside him, doing exactly the same thing.

Jim would write constantly, lyrics, poetry, etcetera, for his mind was always racing with ideas, for the band he had formed in those school days with his friends. It was a way to get all his frustrations out after an unfulfilling day at school. He would reflect on his state of mind, through his words, and he often constructed melodies to fit around those words on his beat-up telecaster, which was fed into a small amp, along with a cheap acoustic kept beside his bed.

It wasn't much, but it was all he had, and it was his.

Jim would listen to a lot of outsider music: The Smiths, Soundgarden, Nirvana, My Bloody Valentine, etcetera. He read books by Jack Kerouac and poetry by Allen Ginsburg among others.

He really liked that whole beat generation thing.

Jim would write constantly about the highs and lows (mostly lows) of being of that age. It was quite a rough time for Jim and his friends being classed as outcasts, for the way they would dress and conduct themselves, brought negative attention from all the cliquey types.

Basically, they were the ones who had to be seen and mostly heard; he always thought of them as idiots with not an original thought in their lacklustre minds.

People thought them strange, the typical outsiders.

But that was okay.

Jim and his friends would jam a lot in Tom Patton's parents' garage. Tom was one of Jim's best friends along with Will McCabe, working on all the material Jim had written.

He would turn in fantastic ideas of hope, love, chaos and death. He was consumed with each of these things.

They also had another good friend, Ben Chambers. He didn't play anything, just liked to sit in and listen to everything that was going on and offer any kind of criticism, constructive or not. He would usually sit there smoking a spliff, while the others jammed.

He was very protective of his friends, as he once punched out one guy for starting some trouble with Will at school. He was suspended for his trouble.

But they were all loyal and looked out for each other through school because of who they were and what with the music they listened to.

Also, Jim being the way he was, he was an easy target for bullying.

After rehearsing, he would have a smoke (weed). It became a sort of ritual after each jam. Then, more often than not, it was down to the local boozer to chat about the rehearsal while at the same time slowly getting more and more drunk, after which they would chat any form of shit that came to them.

They would play a few games of pool and then out to the back garden for a smoke (of both kinds).

That night when he got home, he staggered through the front door as quiet as a herd of stampeding elephants, falling into his mum's flowers, which were located just within kicking distance as he stumbled his first step through into the porch, sending them sprawling.

All the while his dad just sat in the kitchen watching this spectacle lumbering towards him with a cup of tea and a sly cigarette, which he kept secret from the Mrs, as she thought he'd packed up about three years previous.

"Well, look at the state of you. Good rehearsal, was it?" his dad said. A wry smile crept across his face, which turned to a chuckle.

"Yeah, not bad. Got a few things sorted, yer know." His dad just shook his head. "I don't know; you say you practise in Tom's garage, but you always come back absolutely plastered."

Jim laughed. "Yep, weird, innit? Anyway, you better not let Mum catch you smoking; she would have a few things to say," he said with a big drunken grin.

"Right, I'm off to bed, and don't make a bleeding mess."

Jim just nodded while trying to fill the kettle up. Most of the water was spilling into the sink and over the sides.

After making his tea, he stepped out into the garden, the night sky was littered with a million stars as he sat there with his tea, fumbling around in his pockets for his cigarettes. Lighting one, he stared out into the vast blackness, wondering how far it went.

It gave him great ideas for both songs and poems; it really drove his thought process.

Jim sat down on the grass and as the torturing, twisted bleakness rolled round in his head, the panic and darkness set in.

He wrapped both arms around himself, rocking back and forth, wishing this whole thing would just "FUCK OFF" and let him live normally like everyone else.

Looking back to the sky, thinking out loud, he said, "Why me? Why fucking me?"

As the dawn rose to greet the day, Jim woke. His clothes were soaked through from the dew. "Not again."

As he sat up in the cold morning, the cool air lashed around his neck. He shivered as the cold rushed up his wet back.

Luckily it was early enough for his folks not to be up yet. He lit a cigarette, glanced down at the half cup of tea he didn't manage to finish and threw the remainder on the grass.

Jim made his way up to his room unnoticed, undressed and fell back onto his bed. No sooner had he shut his eyes than the alarm kicked in. "Oh shit." It was time to get up for work.

He lay there a while, for he had snoozed the clock like any rational person would. Gathering his bearings, he leaned over to his writing pads, flicking through some of the words he had written, smiling at some and cringing at others.

He had the shower on cold as so to wake him. He thought about the boring day ahead in that godforsaken factory, grinding the soul out every unfortunate person who worked there, except Jim's superior.

Chapter 2

Jim just dreaded going to that place. He always joked to the others who worked there, "I'm depressed enough already; I really don't need this in my life. It will, for certain, drive me to an early grave."

The banter with the other workers was the only thing that really got him through.

Jim, at every convenient time (for him that is, not the company), would sneak off to have a smoke on the fire escape or go and sit in one of the toilet cubicles to read the paper and write. He would always carry a writing pad and a pen for when the time seemed right to go for that unauthorised break.

He was usually questioned by Dan, his supervisor as to his whereabouts. Jim would always answer, "Just went to see a man about a dog," then smile and be gone.

Dan was a lanky streak of piss, who thought himself superior because he had a clipboard.

He would always pander to the factory hierarchy, hanging on their every word like some sort of trained dog.

That evening Jim got a call from Tom that his dad had gotten them a gig at the WMC. It wasn't ideal, but it was a start.

That evening they all got together for a session of music and dope.

While discussing songs for the gig, Ben jumped in.

"Well, you guys have a couple dilemmas."

Will turned around.

"What the fuck are you talking about, Ben?"

Ben just blew a big cloud of marijuana smoke out.

"Right. It's all well and good that you've got this gig, but there are two slight problems." The others just looked at him, quite confused.

"Well, what are they then, Mr Know-it-all?" Tom said.

Ben laughed sarcastically. "Well, you're gonna be playing the Working Men's Club, right?" All nodded.

"And your point is?" Will said, still with that slight confused look on his face.

"What sort of music do they usually have at working men's clubs?" Ben questioned. Jim looked at the others, shrugging his shoulders with them following suit. "Just music, which we have," Tom said.

"Yeah, but only your music," Ben said.

"And?" Jim replied.

Ben shook his head in disbelief.

"Well, who the FUCK is gonna know your songs, you massive bell ends? You are gonna need cover songs, songs that people actually know and also, what are you called?"

Jim just looked stunned then burst out laughing, because Ben was right and because obviously they didn't t have any covers for the set.

"Oh shit, now we've gotta learn a shit load of covers and get a name sorted," Tom said with huge disappointment that they had actually got to think of a name.

Ben reclined back into his chair, his spliff hanging from his mouth, with an over-confident, annoying smile.

Jim looked up and huffed.

"Right, I think we all need to go home and think about a name and songs, especially songs for the older folk who go down these places. Go on YouTube and find some decent songs, and easy ones at that; nothing stupid and complicated."

(As they were not clued up on any of the old stuff, they were quite ignorant in that department.)

So that night they all trawled through different songs, mainly sixties and seventies.

At this time, Jim went into one of his blackest times, feeling the walls closing in on him. Panic screamed through his head as he dived onto his bed, covering his head and crying hysterically.

With the dark shadows enclosing him, he ran to the bathroom and jumped in the shower, fully clothed, his mind racing, a hood of darkness seeping over him.

His mum heard his cries from downstairs and ran up to the bathroom shouting, "Jim, are you okay?" She frantically hit the door, calling downstairs for his dad to come up. His dad raced up and began knocking. "Jim, son, what's going on? Are you okay?"

Then it went silent, but they could hear the shower running. Jim's dad kicked the door in. Jim was curled up under the shower, sobbing uncontrollably. His dad switched off the shower, while his mum grabbed a towel, covering him up, trying to get him out, and took him back to his room. They tried but failed to get anything from him. He went blank and closed his eyes, still shaking. His parents discussed over him that they should get him to a doctor.

Jim's mum rang each of his friends, asking them if he had had an episode like the one she described to them. Each of them said that he did go into some kind of panic attack, but didn't think it too serious because he would level out after a while (after a few spliffs), but obviously they weren't going tell her that. They all agreed that he should see someone to try and sort himself out.

The next day Jim came downstairs getting ready for work. His dad asked if he was okay. He just nodded and said he was fine, then his mum came through and tried to give him a hug, which weirded him out because she had never done that before. He just backed off.

"Oh, Jim, I'm just trying comfort you after last night." A single tear streamed down her face, "I'm fine; don't worry about me. It just sometimes happens. I can deal with it."

He swigged the last of his tea down, grabbed a slice of toast and went out for his bus.

Still feeling some of the strain of the previous night, he got off at the stop before his usual one. He went into the park to gather his thoughts before the test of another dull work day. He rolled up the last of his weed and sat there staring at the sky.

Watching a plane flying overhead, Jim blew a smoke ring that encircled the plane, then it flew off into the clouds. Jim said to himself, "Where you off to today? Somewhere nice, I'm guessing."

Drawing on the last of the spliff, he flicked off the roach into the grass, feeling a lot better now.

Jim was still pondering the thought as he looked up and saw someone walking through the park with a bright blue coat on. As the rain started coming down the person threw over the hood, which was way too big; it flopped over like a veil. Jim thought about the previous night's conversation about naming the band.

And it came to him. Blue Veil Rain. He mulled over it while getting up from the bench and flicking the wet away from the back of his coat. The name stuck with him.

He then texted the others to tell them the name he'd just thought of.

Tom texted back and was all for it; he really liked it. Will was a little unsure. He said it sounded like another band but couldn't think which, but he admitted that he was stuck for a name so agreed.

At work he went down to where the machinists were, all old boys who'd been there since the beginning of time, to question them about the old music and decent songs his band could play for the gig.

They all came out with all the same bands which were popular during the sixties and seventies – The Beatles, The Rolling Stones, The Who, The Kinks, etcetera, reeling off some of the well-known songs from those bands, because everyone would recognise them.

John, one of the old boys, said, "Which club yer playing at?" So Jim told him.

"Aggh, I go there with the Mrs on Fridays and Saturdays. I'll come down and see yer."

Jim thought, "Oh great, old John with his old wife; so it's gonna be full of those types."

Well, truth be told, Jim had never set foot in a WMC before, so it would be a real eye-opener.

All the oldies would be trying to twist, now with their plastic hips and fake knees. He laughed to himself before heading to his office (the toilet cubicle) to have a bit of quiet time and scribble down some lyrics and the song titles of the bands they were just talking about.

Jim texted the rest of the band when he had written down some things to play, to give them a heads up of things they needed work on.

Both texted back almost immediately with approval. Now they needed time to listen to those songs before jamming on them.

Jim felt excitement and apprehension coursing through his entire being, thinking about the gig.

"Is this gig a real gig?" he thought, leaning back against the wall, a smile spread across his face.

There was a knock on the door. "Jim, are you in here?" It was Dan. "Err, yeah, be out in a bit."

"All right, just need a word." Jim heard the door go. He thought, "Oh shit, what does he want?" As he came out, Dan was waiting.

"Mr Osborne wants to see you."

Jim thought, "Oh great; time to get my best poker face on."

While walking to his office, Dan started to question Jim.

"I've noticed you always disappear to the toilet for large amounts of time. What do you actually do in there?"

Jim shook his head. "Well, I do have a weak stomach, if you must know." Dan just glanced at him, a distrustful look etched on his face as if to say, "Yeah, right."

Dan then told Jim that he had informed the boss that he was always disappearing and not getting his work done. Jim glared at him. "You fucking what! Why did you grass me up?"

Dan just looked at him with a sly, smarmy smile.

"Well, why should you take all these breaks while others are working? Anyway, it might give you the kick up the arse you need."

Jim's anxiety started to build, the tension streaming through his whole body, thinking, "Fuck, he's trying to get me the sack, little prick."

As they got to the office of Mr Osborne, the boss, Dan knocked on the door. "Come in." The voice rattled through Jim's soul.

Walking in there was like walking into a Turkish bath, but instead of invigorating steam, the office contained clouds of strong cigar smoke.

Jim gagged. Even though he smoked himself, this was enough to choke out the strongest of smokers. "Agh, Jim, how are you doing?" Mr Osborne said while sifting through some papers and brandishing another stinking cigar. When lit, the plume of smoke given off by the cigar was like a steam engine. (He would succumb to his years of smoking soon after.)

"I'm not too bad. How's yourself?"

Dan looked at Jim, startled at what he just said.

But Osborne laughed. "Not too bad myself, thanks for asking." There was a bit of a pause when Dan the rat chirped up.

"Well, Mr Osborne, I've been keeping tabs on Jim's time-keeping on and off the floor, and it seems to me that Jim would rather spend his time off it, so I just thought you'd like to know."

Osborne was still looking at his papers. "Well, Jim, what do you have to say? Is there any explanation for this?" Jim gave Dan a sharp sideways look.

"I'm sorry that I spend so much time off the floor, but I have a weak stomach, like I've told Dan several times."

The bullshit spilling from Jim's mouth was plain to see, but he thought he was giving the performance of a lifetime.

"Okay, well in future, don't eat any crap food before you come here, then maybe you'll settle down." Jim threw a sarcastic-looking smile towards Dan.

"Thank you, Mr Osborne. I will try in future." Jim nodded.

"Oh, and in future, Daniel, please take your concerns to Mr Johnson. He's your floor manager. I have enough to do, and my time is limited."

Dan held his clipboard to his chest, stunned by what he had heard. "Yes, sir, I will do, but I just thought, on this occasion –"

Dan was interrupted by the dismissive tone of "Goodbye", as Mr Osborne was still deep in his paperwork and never gave him a second look.

On the way back up, Dan was seething at being brought down a peg or two.

"Hey, Jim, you are gonna fuck up again, and you will be caught out." Jim just nodded, his lips pursed.

"Whatever," he said and walked on back. He told nearly the whole floor about the fucking snake and that he'd find a way to get away from him and out of this dump.

That evening at the rehearsal, Jim told them about his day and the fact that that little prick tried to get him the sack.

Tom said, "Oh, fuck him. All he's got is that place and he'll remain there cause he hasn't got the balls to do anything else."

Jim also told them about the conversations he had had with all the old boys who worked there and that most of them went down to that WMC. He explained that he was a bit nervous about playing in front of those guys.

Tom piped up, "Don't worry about it; we've got enough time to get this together and get these songs done. We'll blow them away, I'm that confident."

Jim tried to seem relaxed but was stuttering. He felt an uneasiness about him.

"Well, it's just that I know those guys go down there with their other halves."

But as the days went on, they rehearsed all the time, sharpening those songs they needed to do. They were getting them down pretty quickly.

And the confidence flowed through the rest of them. They knew they were on a massive ride with this guy. Jim had a great aura around him.

Jim stood and gave the most commanding speech.

"If we fuck this up, we are nothing to nobody. We should get it together and get out there and blow this fucker up!" He spoke with complete conviction.

The others were stunned by what Jim had just said, but they understood and knew where he was coming from. At about the same time he was talking, old Ben came strolling in.

"I was listening to that little speech outside. The music sounds great and you've made your case, now fuck em!"

Jim smiled. "Cheers, Ben, means a lot."

Chapter 3

The night of their first gig arrived. Will's older brother Jez gave them a lift in his van.

As they got to the door, the manager of the place greeted them. He was a short, stocky character with a receding hairline and comically long hair at the back, which he brought to the front in a crazy comb-over.

"All right, lads, are you tonight's band then?"

Jim stepped forward. trying to contain his laughter.

"Yep, we are. I'm Jim, and this is William and Thomas."

Both looked at Jim as if to say, "You absolute bastard", for they were not that keen on their names and Jim knew it. He loved to mess with them any chance he got.

Jim turned and winked. Tom gave him the finger.

The manager then asked, "So what are you guys called?"

"Blue Veil Rain," Jim responded.

The manager nodded. "Okay. I'll show you to the stage and you can set up and sound check. The dressing rooms are through the back, just past the bar." He pointed in the direction.

"The sound guy, Chris, isn't here yet, but you can set your stuff up anyway."

They started unloading the van, setting all the gear up on the stage.

A tall, thin set man came bounding towards them.

"Hello, lads, I'm Chris." They shook hands, and Chris asked them their names. He then went over to the control desk to do the sound check.

This was the first time they had ever had one, so they were all pretty nervous, laughing at each other, the tension showing on their faces.

Chris then spoke up. "I take it this is your first gig?" They all nodded.

"That's okay, you'll be fine, just do what I ask, then there will be no problem."

They went through a few songs until they got the sound they needed.

Then they went down to the bar for a pre-gig drink. People started piling in for the night; some of Jim's co-workers were there.

Jim started drinking faster. The nerves were kicking in, and his anxiety levels were rising at a vast rate.

"Guys, I need to step out for a minute."

Will said, "Okay, mate, we'll come with you."

When they got outside, Jim slid down the wall onto his haunches.

"Agh, man, I'm feeling it, and not in a good way – my anxiety is kicking in."

Will, who already had a spliff on, said, "Here, mate, have a grab on that, that'll sort you out." Jim got hold of the spliff, took a couple of big hits on it and held it in to get the maximum effect before letting it all blow out.

He smiled and shut his eyes, trying to compose himself.

"Feeling any better?" Tom asked. Jim nodded, his eyes still closed.

"Yep, not too bad."

Just then, Ben came round the corner.

"Hello, guys, how's it going? What time you starting?"

Will said, "After we've done here." Ben rolled up a spliff of some potent skunk weed, which they passed round. Tom held on it for longer than the others, getting more stoned.

Ben then asked, "Is he okay?" pointing to Jim, who was still down against the wall with his eyes shut.

"Yeah, I'm fine, just felt a little, yer know, out there."

Ben said, "You're all right now though?" Jim just nodded.

At that point, the fire door opened and the manager stepped out.

"All right lads, just coming out for a crafty fag." He sniffed the air. "You been smoking weed out here?"

Tom said, "No, mate, not us. Some lads round there; must be them." The manager gave Tom a sideways look as if to say, "Yeah, right."

They made their way back in. All were feeling pretty good after that smoke. Jim appeared to be a little more confident as they made their way to stage.

Chris was behind the sound desk. Tom made his way behind the drum kit, shaking his head, laughing that he was off it. Will got his bass and Jim his guitar. They re-tuned their instruments before Jim went to the mic. "One, two, one, two." He stuck a thumb up to Chris, and he replied with a thumbs up.

"Hello, we're Blue Veil Rain." Some of the audience clapped while some just stared blankly and others were just carrying on their conversations. Jim said, "One two three four" and they went into The Kinks 'You Really Got Me'.

All the older ones turned round to watch and were starting to get into it, with a few heads bobbing along with the music.

Tom was trying to get his head together, as that feeling was overwhelming him. He was struggling to even hold the sticks, but by some miracle he managed to hang on throughout each song, and it was going okay. A couple of Jim's co-workers signalled to Jim with a positive thumbs up. Which Jim seeing that, he settled in, rolling with the numbers and getting a better reception to each song. All was going really well.

All of sudden they heard the biggest crash. Jim and Will both turned round. Tom was so stoned that he had fallen back over the back of the stage, and there was, unbeknown to them, a five-foot drop behind the curtain, which was obscured by the back-drop curtain. The whole audience were shocked into silence, then a huge roar of laughter erupted. Both Jim and Will fell about laughing.

They went over to the back of the stage and looking down, they saw Tom laying there, surrounded by the remnants of his drum kit. He was holding the back of his neck and was in considerable pain. He looked up and saw Jim and Will looking down at him, laughing hysterically.

Tom looked around, all confused, "What the fuck happened?"

Ben, who was sitting at the bar, had fallen off his stool and was just a mess on the floor.

Jim and Will went down and helped Tom up, picking up the pieces of his drum kit that had fallen off.

Will said still laughing. "You wanna carry on?"

Tom looked at him. "Yeah, okay." He was still on another planet.

Jim went over to Tom. "You massive idiot; are you okay?"

Just then, an inebriated Ben came over.

"Agggh, man, that was amazing!" Tom looked at him with those glazed eyes "Was that part of the show?" Ben said with a huge amount of sarcasm.

Chris came from behind the sound desk and went over and asked Tom if he was okay. Tom nodded; by this time he was laughing about it.

"Right, we'll leave it there, lads," Chris said.

Will then said, "We thought we could carry on."

"No, that'll be all. You were pretty decent, especially for your first time."

Chris knew they were stoned out of their heads, so it was best to call it a night. He then got on the mic.

"Well, that ended a little prematurely so gonna have a disco for the rest of the night. I would like to thank Blue Veil Rain for coming down and playing; hopefully they'll play again soon. Cheers, lads." And so they started shifting all the gear off the stage and back to the van. The disco started in the background, and still there were rolls of laughter around the place. Tom started to feel embarrassed by it now, but after getting a beer down his neck he was soon relaxed and just thought, "Fuck it."

They were hanging at the bar, consuming more drinks, sitting there laughing and messing around and also chatting with family and the people Jim worked with.

Then who should come walking through the door but Dan, the low-life grass. Jim saw him; he had been feeling good up until that point. He necked his beer and ordered a double JD and downed that in one.

Jim was now feeling it, and as he got more inebriated, his mind became darker. He pointed Dan out to Tom and Will.

"There's that prick, Dan, the one who grassed me up. I'm gonna knock his fucking teeth out." Will tried to calm him down, saying that it wasn't worth it.

Jim was getting angrier as he saw Dan swanning around laughing with everyone, trying to be the centre of attention. Some of them laughed along with him, while others tried to ignore him, and when that failed a couple of them pointed towards Jim.

As they were turning their backs on him, Dan looked across at Jim and waved and smiled with a lot of sarcasm.

Dan carried on making his rounds, and when he got round to where Jim was sitting he approached him and said, "Hello, Jim, how you doing?" Dan had clearly had a few and looked like he was on a wind-up.

Jim just glared at him. "No better for seeing you here, you fucking rat."

Dan stepped back and opened his arms.

"Oh, come on, I'm only doing my job. I've just got a load of grief from those bastards over there, telling me I was a grass." Jim turned his back on him and carried on talking with his friends.

Dan tapped Jim on the back.

"Let's not make this personal; let me buy you a drink."

Tom then turned around to Dan.

"Listen, mate, I suggest you get out of his face; he's in no mood for your shit."

But Dan just looked at Tom, shrugged his shoulders and again started tapping Jim on the back. "Oh, come on, Jim, let's put this behind us. Come on; what do you say?" He was still poking at him. Without a word, Jim stood up, turned around and smashed Dan right across the jaw. He sent him flying across some tables. Drinks flew everywhere; people got up and started shouting at the pair of them. Jim then launched himself towards Dan; Will grabbed Jim and told him to calm down then proceeded to drag him away.

The manager of the place came over shouting at Jim that he would never play there again. As Dan was still on the floor holding his face, he was told to leave as well.

They all piled into the van to head back home.

"Fucking hell, mate," Tom said.

Laughing (he was still a bit stoned), Tom lit a cigarette. "I think you knocked him clean out." Jim just stared out of the window. "Well. he deserved it. I don't feel bad at all."

Chapter 4

The next morning, Jim awoke with a mass of anxiety about the night before. He was thinking, "Shit, I've gotta go there tomorrow." So he just lay there. He picked up the acoustic and just started writing about everything that was in his head. He wrote about five songs that day. He needed to get all the shit that was in his head out! And that was the only way he knew. But in turn it created some of the best songs he had ever written.

The next day, the alarm broke the morning. Jim was lying there, just looking at the ceiling, contemplating the day ahead and how it was all going to turn out.

"Well, nothing I can do about it now," he said to himself.

So Jim got up and had a shower, grabbing some breakfast before heading out the door. He took the bus again to the park stop to have his smoke on that same bench, staring into the grey, subdued sky. He felt a kind of alienation, a loneliness driving his ever-fragile mind to a new low. It seemed everyone he saw just didn't notice or raise an eye in his direction, like he was invisible.

As he entered through the factory doors, one of the women machine operators approached him. "Good morning, Jim. Well, I heard what happened Saturday night. Don't worry; he's been asking for a slap for a while now." She was not one to mince her words.

Jim felt an ease come over him, but it didn't last, as he still had to face them upstairs, for they were the ones who were mainly there. He got to the door, took a few deep breaths and went in. A few of the women turned with painted-on smiles at Jim, with good mornings and that, but he could see in their eyes what they were thinking.

Dan was at the other end of the room; he clocked Jim coming in and walked straight up to him.

"Hey, Jim, just to let you know I pressed full charges for the assault on me Saturday, so be expecting a call from the police soon." Then he walked back to where he was working, a smug smile plastered across his face.

Jay, one of the people Jim worked with, said, "Hey, man, how you doing? I heard what happened at the weekend. Well, he's been asking for it for a long time; the guy's a fucking idiot."

Jim just wanted this day to be over. He started work, getting all the things ready for going out that morning. Those words of Dan's plagued his mind; couldn't think straight. He just dropped what he was doing and headed outside on the fire escape for a cigarette.

He texted Will and told him he was feeling like shit being back work and what Dan had said. Will replied, "Don't worry about it; the guy was a smug prick and he deserved it." The text from his friend made him feel a lot better.

Jim texted back that he wanted to try and get some gigs up town and fuck doing covers; he wanted to play original music and also to get out of the place where he worked; it was driving him mad. Will texted back, agreeing with him, but also said that they still needed a couple of covers for the sets. The rest of the day just went on with people asking about what happened, some agreeing and others disagreeing with what he had done. But in the end, he told others who asked, "What can I do now? It's done."

That night while jamming, Jim introduced the band to his new songs. They also picked out a couple of covers to do at gigs, which Will said would break it up a bit, songs that people knew. They picked 'Paranoid' (Black Sabbath) and 'Honky Tonk Women' (Rolling Stones), as they were very apt songs for them to do, with the music they were playing. (With Paranoid being especially apt For Jim).

Just as they were finishing, Ben turned up.

"All right, lads, how's it going?" He looked at Jim. "You all right, Jim? How did it go at work? I guess it was pretty shit." Jim just relayed everything that had happened.

Ben then decided they should all go down the pub; he thought Jim deserved a bit of down time after everything. As they headed down to the pub, smoking and talking about the things they wanted to do with the band, Ben offered his services to be their manager.

Tom just looked at him and burst out laughing. "You, be our manager? You can't even get yourself out bed and to work on time.'

They all laughed and took the piss. Ben chirped up, "Thinking about it, I guess you're right." As they entered the pub, Ben saw one of his other friends, Rob, whom Jim and co didn't really like. They thought he was too full of himself, so they went on to the bar.

Looking round were two guys playing pool. They were regulars in that pub, and they were also known drug dealers that dealt out of the pub, but landlord didn't bat an eyelid; they would throw him a few hundred to not say anything.

Jim asked the others if they fancied a game of pool and they all agreed, so Jim went over and put money on the side. Then one of them spoke up. "All right, mate."

Jim nodded. "Yeah, fine." The other guy asked them if they fancied a game of doubles. Jim said, "Yeah I will, I'll just ask the others." So grabbing their drinks, they went over and introduced themselves.

They said they had seen them around.

They were Darren Williams and Zack Graham. Daz was loud and very full of himself. On the flip side Zack was quiet and reserved. Both had a reputation for violence when needed; all part of the game they were in.

As they played, Will spoke up. "Er, have you guys got any gear?"

Daz looked up from his shot. 'Yeah – how much you want?" and he followed up with, "Aren't you the ones who played the Working Men's Club the other night, and the drummer fell off the back of the stage?" He chuckled.

(Jim had mentioned they were in a band called Blue Veil Rain.)

Tom put his head down, totally embarrassed. Jim said, "Yep, that's us, and that's him," pointing to Tom, all laughing.

Tom just shook his head. "Whose shot is it anyway?" he said, trying to change the subject.

Then Will said, "Yep, not our finest moment. So how about this gear then?" also trying to change the subject.

"Got twenty pounds? Okay; go to the toilets. I'll be in in a bit."

So Will went in, then Daz followed and they made the deal. "Hey, do you guys take speed or anything like that?"

Will stood there, rolling a spliff. "Err, no just smokers."

"Well, if you guys want any, give us a shout; I'll sort you a gram each."

Will nodded. "Yeah, will do."

As they went out, Zack said, "Daz, your shot, mate," and Will went over to Jim and Tom. "Any of you guys wanna get some speed? He says he can get some." Jim's ears pricked up. "Yeah, definitely."

So Will said to Daz, "We're up for that, man."

At that time, Ben had re-joined them and was introduced, Tom let Ben know the situation, that they were getting some speed, a gram each. Ben nodded his approval; he was up for it too. Daz played his shot. "Cool. I'll leave it under that cushion. Point to one of the chairs and you just leave the money; it will be another twenty pounds," he said with a wide grin.

After they did the exchange, Jim and co went to the toilet to take it. The initial take was a horrible, sour taste, and they all gagged. They got rid of the cellophane wrappers and went back in. Daz and Zack both grinned at them as if to say, "You're gonna be fucking buzzing in a bit." As they all carried on playing pool, the effects started kicking in: they felt rushes flowing through them and that was it, they were up.

Jim's jaw started to contort. He couldn't help it. The others started laughing at him but then it happened to them. Both Daz and Zack fell around in hysterics at the sight before them. Jim and company decided to adjourn to the garden, because they thought they were making too much of a scene. They sat at one of the tables, unable to sit still; they were twitching like mad. Jim said, "This is the best feeling ever."

Jim would go on to take more, even when his friends stopped. That evening, when the effects wore off, Jim felt very uneasy within himself. He couldn't understand; the speed had made him feel so good, but now he was feeling the comedown. And with his mind not exactly in the greatest place, the effects from the comedown were exacerbated.

Chapter 5

The next morning, while Jim was having breakfast, his mum told him that he had an appointment at the doctor's that afternoon, to discuss what was going with him.

He just sat there not saying a word; his mind was still scrambled from the previous night. But then he spoke up. "Yeah, whatever." Without saying another word he got up to go to work.

The day rolled on in the same way. Jim was longing to get his band into town, to play the places they all knew. It was time they got out there. They had the songs already and just needed the right place to play.

Jim had previously said to the others how they should go up town and have words with some of the venues, for they hadn't been to any of them yet but had heard from others about the decent places to play. So they made plans for that Saturday to go and have a look; there were a couple of bands playing at one of the venues they had heard a lot about, the Phoenix. They planned to score some more speed off Daz and Zack for the night. So Jim contacted Daz about getting some and agreed to meet up at the venue.

The night came. All were quite excited about it and a bit nervous about talking to somebody about arranging a gig, because obviously they hadn't done it before.

They started at the local for a few, just to take the edge off how they felt, then caught the bus into town. They got there for eight p.m. but the bands didn't start till nine thirty, so they had plenty of time to look around. It was a venue where you had the pub in the front and gigs were in the back; a juke box was located near the bar. They flicked through the selections of music. There was a lot of sixties and seventies stuff plus more of the bands they listened to, which made them grin.

Led Zeppelin's 'Black Dog' was playing.

They walked through the back door which led to the stage area and just stood there, staring at the stage, lights filling the whole room, the microphones set up at the front and all the instruments set up. Jim felt a tension filling him, as if it was he was he who was playing that night. Will and Tom were talking about how great it would be to be up there.

Just then, Jim felt a tap on the shoulder. It was Daz and Zack. "All right, lads. You made it then."

They all nodded. "Yeah, fucking great being here, love it," Tom shouted over to them. He had to, as the music was loud; it was the pre-gig music. Daz told them they had got the stuff on them and that they should go to the toilet to make the deal.

And one by one they took it, that horrible sour taste, all gagging, automatically swigging their beers to get rid of the taste. They all decided to adjourn to the bar for some drinks just before the bands came on.

Just then they heard the sound of a guitar being strummed and the high-pitch sound of feedback. Chills ran down Jim's neck. He grabbed his beer and moved quickly to the stage area. There on stage was the band, looking so cool. Jim just shook his head and took a big swig of his beer and blew out a deep breath. The excitement was mounting, and then Will and Tom came in and jumped on Jim's shoulders. "Yeahh, fucking yeeaahh" screamed Will, right down Jim's ear. But Jim didn't mind; he was just mentally in the zone.

As they were watching, they noticed someone waving from the side of the venue. As the light splashed on the wall they saw it was Ben; he was jumping up and down and waving towards them. He came down from where he was standing and was dancing through everyone, holding his pint above his head.

"Hello, guys, how long you been down here?"

Jim put his arm around Ben, cupping his hand around his ear.

"About an hour. Fucking amazing!" Both Will and Tom were trying to talk to Ben through all the loud music, by which time the speed was starting to kick in. They started dancing erratically.

Ben shouted to Jim, "Are you guys speeding?" Jim just looked at him and produced a massive grin.

Ben asked if they had any more. Jim said, "No, but I can get some if you want some." Ben smiled and nodded. Jim told him that Daz and Zack were in the bar and that they had some. So Ben scurried off to find them. A few minutes later he was back and produced the cellophane bag with the disgusting-tasting powder in there. Ben then lapped it up, and the twisted expression appeared on his face as it hit his taste buds.

It was a great night, and after the last band had finished, they started to leave.

Walking through the bar area, Jim heard his name being shouted. It was Zack; he waved them over. As they approached, Daz spoke up. "You had a good night then?"

They all said "Yeah, it was amazing."

Zack was talking to a big guy behind the bar. "Right, lads, this is Tony. He sorts out all the bands here; he can sort you out."

They all grinned and said, "All right, mate, how's it going?"

Shaking hands, they introduced themselves to Tony. Zack then spoke up.

"Yeah, we've told Tony all about you and we think you'd be perfect playing here. I also told him about your gig at the WMC."

They all looked at Tom, who just blew out his cheeks.

"Yeah, I'm the one who fell off the stage." Tony laughed and said he'd heard about it.

"I'll sort you lads out with a support slot; I will let you know." He took Jim's number and said he'd be in touch. Ben suddenly appeared, got Will in a headlock and knuckled the top of his head.

"Yeah, boyz" Ben said in the style of Public Enemy's Flavur Flav.

They were all buzzing from the comment Tony had said about the support slot. They then went on to one of the clubs in the town; they heard the distinctive tunes of the music they were all into and felt totally at home.

The rest of the night just became a blurry haze. They were still buzzing from the band they had just seen and the drugs. Jim awoke at the side of his bed, thinking, "How the fuck did I get back here?" He couldn't remember a thing.

This in turn started to cause him massive anxiety just trying to think about the previous night. He got up, went to the bathroom, washed his face and just sat on the bath, trying to figure it out. "I hope I didn't cause any shit." He started to shake, so he went back to his room to call Tom.

"Hello mate, how the fuck did I get back last night?"

Much to his relief Tom just said, "Agh, we just got a taxi; you were fucking out of it mate, trying get credit for more speed." He laughed.

"Really? What did they say?"

Jim's voice was etched with a nervous tone.

"Oh, they just told you to calm down and that you had had enough. Funny that, coming from a pair of dealers," Tom said.

"Right, so I didn't make a massive twat of myself?" Jim said.

There was a pause.

"Well, you did; you tried to get off with some girl who was with her boyfriend. Fortunately, he was at the bar. We tried to drag you away and she was telling you to fuck off."

Tom laughed; he then told Jim he had to go and would call him later. As Jim went downstairs, he heard his folks in the kitchen. He was thinking, "Oh fuck, they're up." He walked in with his head down.

Then his dad said, "Here he is. God, how much did you put away last night? I think it's the worst I've ever seen you." He talked in sarcastic tones. His mum was less than impressed.

"Why do you feel the need to get in those kinds of states? It's absolutely stupid."

Jim didn't say a word. His mind was racing from all that Tom had said, and he felt he couldn't face anyone today and that he might as well call off the rehearsal. Then his mum said, "Oh Jim, I've made an appointment with the doctor for Monday."

Those words rang out, as if he had done something wrong. It did not feel helpful – just the opposite. Then Jim just said,

"Okay, when?" While making his dad's breakfast' his mum said, "Tomorrow, five o'clock. I've made it so you can go after work."

That comment didn't sit well with Jim – not the doctor but work. He went outside, down to the bottom of the garden to have his morning cigarette. His mind started to calm as he smoked – each drag was bliss. Looking into the sky, he wished he could just get out of his situation. After he finally got ready, he was feeling a whole lot better and called off the idea of cancelling the jam, so he got his stuff together and headed over to Tom's. Will was just arriving as he got there.

"Hello Jim. How you feeling? You were totally wankered last night." Will winked and laughed.

"Yeah, I know. Apparently I tried to get off with some girl, Tom told me this morning.

Then Will just carried on. "Yeah, and her boyfriend was at the bar," he said, still laughing. Jim just shook his head and walked into Tom's garage for the rehearsal. Ben turned up as usual, to just sit there, smoke and criticise. And also to take the piss out of Jim like the others, but Jim was getting fed up with it all. "If all you lot are gonna do is take the piss then I'm going." Then he just sat down, his mood clouding over. The others apologised and said that they didn't mean it. But Jim was still reeling in his head from the previous night's exploits. He was trying to get his shit together. He couldn't handle all the bullshit.

"Yeah, I'm okay, thanks," Jim said in a low tone.

Ben went over and put his arm over Jim's shoulder. "Jim. mate, we are sorry for that."

Jim nodded. "Yeah, it's fine, I am okay."

He got up and grabbed his guitar. "Come on then, you wankers, fucking do it."

They got all the songs together for the set. Ben looked at the set list and thought they should do a cover just to get the audience interested, just something they knew.

All in agreement, they had a think about it and one of the songs they knew and could play quite well was 'Paranoid' by

Black Sabbath, which was with Jim, becoming one of his favourite songs.

So that was what they all agreed to play at the start of every rehearsal, just so it became natural for them to do it.

Chapter 6

The next day the dreaded alarm kicked in. Jim rolled over to snooze it, just to get that extra time in bed. He felt that sunken, heavy feeling in his head, as though it was made out of lead. The room always became darker, sounds echoing from downstairs, the familiar sounds he always associated with work. As he managed to drag himself up, he looked at the set list and it gave him hope that he would make it out of that depressing environment. He felt quite good, but not even that could quell that feeling weighing heavily on him, the black hood that enveloped him. After the same routine, getting off the bus early and into the park, he felt a difference about going in, that something was going to change.

Everyone was at their workstations, busy doing the same thing all day, every day. Jim just sat down at the place he worked from and stared out at those people. He felt an overwhelming sense of disdain and hatred for those in his eye line.

Look at all those people doing the same thing, then back home doing the same fucking thing. No difference in their pathetic lives, nothing achieved, only the same machines, same programmes each night, and he wouldn't put it past them to have the same fucking dinners. The whole thing was building up in Jim's fragile mind, and then he saw Dan. Fuck me, I'd rather be dead then be that cretin, sucking up to anyone just to get a bit more power. So Jim just crossed that line and that was enough, he was finished. So he got up and went over to Dan.

"Oi, Dan," Jim shouted over to him. "Come here." As Dan walked over to him, Jim just stood there and laid it all out.

"Right then, you fucking weasel, this is the last time you'll see me. I'm handing in my resignation. I can't sit by and see my whole world just fall by the wayside in this fucking dump and have to see your smug arrogant face day by day. Death seems to be a better option than this. But I've got things I wanna do with my life, so here's a big fuck you!" He walked off. Dan stood there, gobsmacked, and watched as Jim got his coat and went into the manager's office to give him the news. He said his farewells to the others, the ones he actually spoke to, and was gone. Outside, Jim leaned against the wall, lit a cigarette and laughed hysterically. He had finally done it; he had broken away. He felt a massive weight lift from his shoulders. "Right," he thought, "how to break it to my folks?"

That evening, he went down to get his dinner. He sat there, puzzling over what to say.

"Right, I've got something to tell you." Both his parents looked at each other with faces showing alarm bells ringing.

"I quit my job today; I couldn't face it any more. It was driving me insane."

His mum dropped her knife and fork as his dad kept on eating. "So what are you going to do now?" his mum quipped.

"I'm not sure. I'll find something."

His mum stared at his dad. "Well, are you going to say something?"

"What can I say? I quit my first job. He's still young; he'll find something."

Jim's mum shook her head and looked at his dad as if to say, thanks for the backup. "Well, tomorrow you're going to go out and find something if it takes you all day."

Jim just sat there. "Yep, will do."

"Oh, by the way, did you go to the doctor's appointment?" his mum said, still annoyed. Jim froze and thought, "Shit, I knew there was something else I had to do today."

"I completely forgot all about it. I'm sorry." Jim sat there, waiting for the backlash.

But nothing came. His mum finished up and went into the living room to watch her TV. She shut the door as the theme tune came on from her favourite show.

His dad spoke up. "Don't worry about it. I've worked in those factories; by god, they are enough to drive you off a cliff." His dad had a way with words.

"I'll make you another appointment and you better not forget. You really need to sort out what's going on up there," he said, digging his finger into the side of Jim's head.

Jim agreed. "We're getting a gig down at the Phoenix bar soon. That's where we were on Saturday. We got speaking to the guy who promotes the music down there; he said he was gonna give us a shot."

His dad looked at him and nodded. He obviously knew where Jim's heart was – it was in music.

"I've been writing a lot of songs, and I've been working on them with the band; they're coming together nicely." Jim just wanted some recognition from his folks that this was it. He had felt a massive screw-up through school and now with him quitting his job.

His dad got up. "I'm sure you have, and I know you believe in what you're doing, but you still have to find something to get you through. I mean you still need to find a job."

Jim sat there, a little disappointed. He had been expecting a little more from his dad in the form of recognition. He felt quite dejected by his dad's response. Deep down, Jim always wanted to do right by his dad but felt he was never good enough. He also felt that in turn this could have contributed to his mental health issues. He didn't know for sure – it was just a theory. The next morning his mum came into his room and reminded him to go up town and look for a new job.

"I can look online, mum; it's not all job centres nowadays."

"I know that, but I don't want you sitting here all day doing nothing and then pretending that you've been looking for work."

"As if I would," Jim said sarcastically.

His mum just glared at him. "If only I could believe that. Anyway, I'm off to work; some of us have to."

Jim looked out of his window. The weather echoed his mood – dark clouds and rain. He fell back on his bed, grabbed his acoustic and note pad and began working on some new stuff, after which he wrote a couple of poems about life and the way he saw things in the bleakness of it all. The words became blurry as he was writing. He woke up and looked at his phone – he had been asleep for a couple of hours. "Shit!" he said. He got on his phone and trawled through the listings: they seemed to all be the same. Office work, warehouse work, some factory stuff, etcetera. He then spotted an ad for the music shop up town. He thought that would be ideal, so he got the phone number and called them up straight away. After speaking to the owner, he arranged an interview for the next day. Jim thought that wasn't too bad, getting an interview more or less straight away.

"Now where was I?" He looked back over the songs and poetry he had been writing before he passed out. He also called on his friends to tell them about the interview. They were all like, "Oh yeah? Get us some discount stuff."

Jim said, "I haven't got the fucking job yet, and here you all are asking for discounts. If anybody's gonna get any discount it's me; I'm the one gonna be fucking work there." He laughed. When his folks got back, he told them all about the interview. His mum was really impressed with him for actually doing it. And his dad was equally impressed, saying that would be the ideal job because obviously there would be people going in with the same aspirations as his. And he could make some contacts. Jim then went into the garden to have a spliff. He had to go down to the bottom, away from the kitchen, because the window was always open, and his parents frowned on all that sort of stuff.

They believed one toke from a joint and you were hooked.

As far as he could remember, he actually felt good about himself. That was not to say those demons were not there. But he managed to keep them at bay, for the time being.

He was also a jamming that night, so that was doubly cool. His dad had also informed him that he had re-booked the doctor's for the next day and same time, and this time he needed to be there.

Chapter 7

The next day arrived. Jim woke up very apprehensive. He thought he should be feeling great about this interview, but doubts plagued his mind, a voice telling him he wasn't going to get the job and to just give up. He buried his head into his pillow, shouting for those fuckers in his head to go away and leave him alone. He thought about the day ahead and that if he didn't get the job, what he would do? He thought about the doctor's and that he needed to go and try and sort himself out. So many scenarios were flying through his mind; he was spinning and felt he couldn't stop. He once again fled to the bathroom, splashed cold water on his face and looked into the mirror. All he thought was, "Are you good enough? Do you think you can do it? Do you think you will fail?" And it was all heading towards, "No, you're not good enough; you will fail; why bother?" Jim sat with his head in his hands, trying to shake this negative feeling.

He got up and went downstairs. His mum had laid out a shirt and tie for his interview. Jim looked at them with disdain.

"Oh, I forgot about the formalities of the job interview, but in this day and age, is it really necessary?"

His mum said, "Well, you've got to look smart. You can't go in looking like you always do in scruffy jeans and a T-shirt." Jim shrugged his shoulders. He then got his tea, grabbed his clothes and went up to get ready.

While he was getting ready, his phone rang. It was Tony from the Phoenix bar. "Hello, Jim, Tony here, I hope I've not caught you at a bad time?"

Jim said, "No, not at all," while trying to button his shirt.

"Yeah, anyway, I've got a band coming in Saturday night, so if you're up for it, the support slot's yours."

Jim freaked out. "Yes! Definitely we'll have it!"

Tony said, "Nice one, mate. Be down for sevenish for a sound check. Cheers for that – see you Saturday."

Jim nearly jumped through the ceiling he was so happy. He called up Tom and Will straight away to tell them the news. They were equally ecstatic. Jim then called up Ben and told him the news and that they were going to meet later for a few beers to celebrate.

Ben was equally pleased for them and told Jim they deserved it. Jim caught the bus into town. He wandered down the high street, staring into all the offices and at all the people, who were staring blankly into their computer screens. Jim wondered how they could do that day in, day out, just constantly looking into those screens and talking to those irritating people on those headsets.

Jim shook his head, thinking, "That would just cave my head in. I suppose just like factory work, really," was his other thought. As he approached the shop, he saw all the instruments in the window and also some advertisements from people looking for bands, bands wanting people, guitar lessons, etcetera.

Jim walked in and saw an array of different instruments. Wow. To be able to work with all these guitars on view all the time was his idea of heaven. A tall man in his mid-fifties came out from the back. He spotted Jim looking at all the guitars. "Hello, what's can I dos for you?"

Jim was still scoping out the guitars. "Hello, I'm Jim Staley; I've come for the interview."

The man came from around the counter. "Hello, I'ms Terry; nice to meets you. Shall's we go in the back and have a chat?" Jim nodded, trying not to laugh at this guy's speech impediment, thinking, is this really how this guy talks, adding s's after nearly every word? Jim knew it was going to wear thin after a while, but for now he found it funny, even though he didn't outwardly show it. But to Jim he seemed all right.

"So then's, how's are you? Doing okay?" Terry asked Jim, trying to make him as comfortable as possible.

"Yeah, not bad," Jim responded.

"So, whys do you wants to work in a music shop? Are you's a musician, in a band?" Terry questioned.

Jim felt distracted by Terry's voice. "Err, yeah, I'm in a band and that. I previously worked in a factory but felt my life was going nowhere in that place." Jim's head lowered as he told Terry.

Terry listened. "Yep's, I gets what you mean's. I worked in a factory once, ands yes, it is souls-destroying."

Jim replied in full agreement with him. Then Jim said, "So, if I get the job, any chance of discounts?" He gave and sly grin and chuckled.

Terry laughed along with him and called him a cheeky bastard.

Then Terry offered Jim a cup of tea while asking him questions about any experience he had in retail, handling a till, etcetera, to which Jim replied that he hadn't. He told him what the work would consist of: taking in deliveries, dealing with customers, etcetera. Terry liked Jim from the off; he liked his cheeky attitude but also found him quite shy and reserved.

He gave Jim the job but on a temporary basis; he would see how Jim worked out with the workload and how he would deal with customers. Jim would also get to know and understand information on each instrument. Jim agreed and said he would not let Terry down.

Terry said, "Okays then; I'll see's you Monday and get you going."

Jim was excited by this and celebrated by buying a big bag of weed and numerous drinks. He contacted his folks and told them, then called his mates. Jim waited around town until it was time to get the bus to the doctor's. He smoked a cigarette before he went in; his nerves were getting the better of him, trying to figure out what to say to the doctor.

He went in, spoke to the receptionist and sat down. The surgery was a very cold-looking place, all pale blue walls. It had a very old feel to it, and a musty smell lingered which made Jim feel quite sick.

He was then called in. "Aghh, hello, you must be Mr Staley. So what can I do you for?" Jim sat down. He frowned at the doctor's question; he didn't know where to begin.

The doctor just said, "Okay, I know why you're here. I spoke to your mother and she let me know all the details, but I just wanted to make you relaxed, so you could open up and tell me first-hand how you are feeling."

Jim nodded, took his coat off and reeled off everything he felt and what he did to try and handle it. The doctor took notes and told Jim that a lot of people who suffer with some kind of mental illness often self-medicate, to try and numb those feelings.

He said he was glad that Jim had something to fall back on. When he got in those dark places, his music and poetry would be good therapy, as he could write down everything he felt, get it all out. So he offered Jim some numbers of councillors and prescribed him some anti-depressant medication. Jim thanked him and went down to the pharmacy, which was located next door, to get his medication. He swallowed one of the pills then headed to meet his friends. They met at their local pub and all congratulated him on the new job. Tom again talked about discounts. Jim just shook his head and laughed. He spotted Daz and Zack at the pool table as per usual and went over to score some weed.

He told them about the job interview.

"Nice one, mate. I suppose this job will be more up your street than that fucking factory job," Daz said. Jim agreed. Zack then reached into his pocket and dug out a nice big bag of weed. "Here you go; call it a congratulations present."

Jim's eyes lit up. "Wow, thanks a lot; much appreciated." Jim then said in a lowered tone, "Any chance of some speed? I've got a twenty for you."

Zack reached into another pocket and brought out four grams of speed.

"Here yer go, lad. Gonna have to charge you for this one, I'm afraid."

Jim smiled and nodded. "Yep, wasn't expecting any more freebies. Well I wasn't expecting this freebie," he said, lifting up the weed. He then returned to Will, Tom and Ben and went out into the garden to skin up. As they were getting nice and loaded, Jim then produced the speed. "And this is for afters." They all broke into laughter.

Tom then spoke up about the gig on Saturday (which was the next night) down at the Phoenix. "Well, I'm really looking forward to the gig tomorrow. Anybody know the name of the band we're supporting?"

Jim then said, "No, the guy didn't tell me; I should have asked really. But oh well, we'll find out soon enough."

Ben said he might be a bit late for the gig, as he had promised his other mate, Rob, that he would help him with his car, and would be down after. Jim and the others didn't really like Rob. They thought him a bighead, and Rob would take the piss out of Jim and the others, which Ben would relay back to them. Rob thought Jim was neurotic and that the others were just complete stoners and a waste of time. But Ben would always pull him up on it and tell him to shut up, as they were also his friends.

Chapter 8

That night, Jim sat in his room, trying to cope with the comedown; the speed was now wearing off. He felt extremely agitated, pacing round the room. He put on some relaxing music to try and calm his nerves and went for 'Shoot You Down' by The Stone Roses, 'That Joke Isn't Funny Anymore' by The Smiths and 'Polly' by Nirvana.

They were not the most uplifting but suited his needs. He drifted off into some wild and vivid dreams. He woke the next morning, feeling very paranoid and trembling, his nerves shot. He reached over and took one of his pills.

His phone went off:. it was Ben

"Hello, Jim, how's it going?" Jim told him he was feeling a bit out of sorts but was going to be ready for the gig later that night. Ben told Jim that he had met a girl from his work and was going to bring her down. And Jim being Jim, he wound Ben up about it with, "What? You've met a girl? Does she carry a white stick?" and other words to that effect. But said that he was glad he had found someone and that he wished Jim could.

"It might sort my head out," Jim said.

Ben said, "Man, you're too intense for any relationship, but I mean that in the most honest way, mate. You need to chill out a bit." Jim thought this was a bit harsh. He knew he was right but didn't let him know that. Jim just said, "You cheeky bastard." They both laughed and Jim told Ben he'd better go and get himself sorted for later on.

"Don't want to be flipping out at the gig," Jim said with a chuckle.

Ben laughed his cheeky laugh and told him to get those happy pills down his neck. He then again congratulated Jim on his new job.

"Cheers, mate. Right, I will catch you later."

That day they went over to Tom's house to jam in his garage, just to get things right and go through the set list. This had now

Black Sabbath's 'Paranoid' as the opener. They chose that one as they thought it would get them some attention; people's heads might turn with a familiar song, especially a rock classic like that. After the session they made their way into the garden for a smoke and to discuss the upcoming gig. Jim then went on to tell them about Ben calling him and letting him know about his new girlfriend. (When I say new, this was his first.)

You see, those four had never really had what you would call luck in the ladies' department. They were either too immature or too fucked up for any of them to get anyone to take them seriously. They seemed to lack appeal.

Will then went on. "How the hell did that little runt get anyone, especially before me?" Will was going on about his own self-importance, how he assumed he would be the first one to get a girl.

Tom shook his head. "Well, Ben's a lot better looking than you, Will; you're an ugly bastard." Jim spat out his drink, laughing. As the evening drew on it was time to get everything down to the venue. Tom's brother now took them down in his van, since neither of them could drive. When they got there, it was dead apart from a few punters drinking in the front bar. They made their way into the back and were met by Tony.

"Hello, lads. Are you ready for tonight?"

They all said, "Yeah," and "Kind of," etcetera. The nerves were starting to kick in. Jim was shaking; the anxiety was overwhelming. He dropped one of his pills, hoping it would sort him out. Tom asked Tony who they were supporting.

"Didn't you see the posters at the front?"

They were like, "What posters?"

Tony shook his head and laughed. "Go to the front bar – there're a few posters for tonight on there."

They went back through and spotted them on the wall. They were in awe of what they saw. Their name on a poster in town. The other band were called Trojan Knights. They looked at each other.

Then Will said, "Trojan fucking Knights? What kind of name's that?"

They all laughed at what they thought was a ridiculous name, made their way back through and grabbed a few drinks, then went back out to unload their gear. As they were lugging their stuff through, the other band were up on the stage for the sound check. They were playing old seventies glam tunes. They looked at each other, nodding their heads to the music.

Will then said, "Hmm, not too bad; still a shit name though."

Then Ben turned up with his girlfriend and introduced her to the lads. Ben then asked, "Is that the headliner?" looking up to the stage.

Tom said, "Yeah; have you seen their name?" Ben said he hadn't.

Will then chipped in. "They're called Trojan Knights," he said while shaking his head. "I mean, come on,' what sort of names that?" Will's face had the look to go with his comment. Ben found it hilarious.

It was now their turn for a sound check, kicking in with a couple of their own songs.

The other band was watching them play, and after they had finished a couple of them went up and introduced themselves.

"Hello, like your set, man. I'm Kes, and this is Damon. We were really impressed with those songs you just did; they your own?"

Jim nodded and said, "Thanks, we really appreciate it."

Kes then said, "We heard this is your first proper gig?"

Will spoke up. "Well, we had a working men's club gig, but we'll say no more about that." He winked at Tom and Tom then flipped him off with his middle finger. "Agh, like that, was it?" Damon said with a smile on his face. "Well, everyone's been there; don't worry about it. Learning curve and all that."

They were shaking hands and wishing each other luck when over came their lead singer, striding across the floor like he was god's gift, throwing his hair back like he was in a shampoo ad.

"Hi, guys, I'm Jesse, Jesse Knight, the lead vocal of Trojan Knights." He stood there with his hands on his hips, wearing Rod Stewart-type leopard-print leggings and a crop top, with cowboy boots and hair straight out of your typical eighties metal band.

It was a sight to behold. Jim couldn't help but laugh, but he made it sound like a cough, he thought.

"Oh my fucking God!" He then said, "So I'm guessing the band is named after you?"

"Certainly is; it's my band. Well, I just came over to say, since this is your first gig, you might need a few pointers on stage presence."

They all looked at each other. Tom just shook his head. "No, we're fine, mate, we don't need any gimmicks and stage presence; we just let the music do the talking." The sarcasm was flowing nicely. Will sniggered. Jesse looked at Will and then glared at Tom.

"You definitely need stage presence to give the audience something good to look at; you know, a certain flare. So just watch what I do and take some pointers. I've been doing this for years, so I know what I'm talking about."

Again Jim just stood there grinning, trying hard to contain his laughter. "Okay, mate, we'll try and take some pointers off you and see where it goes." The sarcasm was screaming from Jim's mouth.

Jesse just said, "Okay, well guys, have a great gig and we'll see you after and I'll give you my honest opinion." He then turned and walked back.

Will said, "What the fuck was that!" while giggling. "Remember, guys, to take pointers from Jesse Knight – he knows his shit." Jim and co headed back to the bar, still laughing, one of the other band members was sitting having a lonesome pre-gig drink. Jim took a stool next to him.

"Hello, mate. I'm Jim; I'm with the band supporting you tonight. We've just had our sound check. I thought you guys sounded pretty cool."

"Agh. Thanks. Man. I saw you guys – you've got a nice sound."

Jim thanked him and said about meeting a few guys from his band.

"Yeah, I saw you talking to some of the other guys. They're cool, but on the flip side I need to outright apologise for our singer. He is a complete show-off who generally thinks he's bigger than he actually is. He fucking winds me up, but we tolerate him. Anyway, I'm Pete, the drummer."

Jim just laughed. "Yeah, the first two were sound, but then he came over and we all thought, wow, what a dick. Also, is the band named after him?"

"Unfortunately yes, and he's never let us forget it. We had a draw of straws for who would name the band, because we couldn't decide. And he won" Pete shook his head, laughing. He then politely asked if he could have a bit of his own time. It was what he did before gigs to get him ready. Jim obliged and said both bands ought to get together for a drink after.

Pete said, "Yeah, maybe."

They made their way to stage. The humming of the amps was an exciting sound to them. Jim had thought about this moment for so long and now it was here. Jim approached the microphone. He could feel the sweat under his arms. His clammy hands shook, and he didn't know if he was going to make it. He took a deep breath. "Hello, we're Blue Veil Rain. How is everyone feeling? Okay!"

There were about ten people in the audience but they were very receptive to Jim's call and answered with yeahs, whoops and a couple of whistles. Bursting in with Black Sabbath's "Paranoid", and the crowd cheered, and a couple of people started dancing. This was very encouraging. Jim took the mantle and ran with it, playing erratically and jumping up and down. Will and Tom just looked at each other as if to say, "What the Fuck!" but then they were driven by Jim's energy to play harder.

Ben got to the front of the stage, jumping up in front of Jim's face and making all kinds of weird faces, which Jim found hilarious. And the mosh pit was rocking with all these drunken people really digging the sound and vibe. Jesse Knight looked at them with complete disdain. He turned to Kes.

"Oh dear, look at those amateurs; they haven't really got it, have they?" Kes just looked at him, shook his head and walked off. After they had finished, they got a resounding round of applause from the audience, which had swelled to about fifty by this time. Jim was really taken aback by the numerous people who were digging their sound; he thought this was a proper gig up town in a proper music venue. They had broken the ice.

Pete went to them as they were coming off and told them how good he thought they were and especially for their first gig, as did the other members. All apart from Jesse Knight – he approached them with a slow, sarcastic clap.

"Not bad, guys, for your first time, but you need a stage presence, an alter ego; you look, just too plain." Jim and the others were really not impressed by this idiot's attitude. Jim exclaimed, "Do you mean and big fucking ego, like yours?" He gave a sarcastic smile. Jesse didn't hear him, and as the band mounted the stage, he went into the back dressing room. The others started getting themselves together. Their instruments then burst into what turned out to be an intro. They had their own personal intro; was all very pretentious.

But the music was pretty good. It was like seventies glam, a bit Mark Bolan-ish. Then suddenly out from the back he emerged. And what a sight befell them. Jesse was now in his stage wear; he was like a chicken in makeup. He wore a feathered jacket, silver flares and stack-heeled boots. Jim and the others stood aghast at the sight, and Ben just blurted out, "What the fuck does he look like?" They all laughed between them, which Will, Tom and Ben did, but Jim held his composure, all the while laughing inside. He wanted to show them a bit of respect. The crowd took to it; well, I guess most of them were there to see them anyway. They watched for a bit longer then adjourned to the bar, where Daz and Zack were holding court with a bunch of people they obviously knew.

"Good gig, lads," Daz said as they approached the bar. They all smiled and thanked him. The rest of the people who were there all agreed.

Zack then piped up, "But I don't think much to that fucker up there now. What the fuck does he look like?" They all laughed.

Will then said, "He is a big-headed twat. He told us we were amateurs, like he was some sort of major rock star and that." He shook his head while taking a drink from his pint.

As the night went on, they scored some more drugs. They went outside to have a smoke and ended up with some bags of speed on the courtyard table in the garden and snorted it all, within which time they were buzzing again with those facial twitches. They heard the Trojan Knights announce it was their last song and went back inside for it. All bounced around to the song, for it was a cover of David Bowie's, "Jean Genie", a song that everyone knew and so the place was rocking. As they dismounted the stage, Jim went up to them and told them that they had had a great set.

Jesse came down last, playing the ultimate rock star. "Nice gig, man," Jim said to him.

Jesse turned to Jim. "Well, that's how you do it. I saw your set, and you need to work on your stage presence. Take me as a role model if you wish."

Jim, buzzing from all the booze and drugs, couldn't control himself.

"Who the fuck do you think you are? You come out dressed like a fucking psychedelic chicken, poncing around like you think you own fucking everyone. Your own band thinks you're a massive dick. So wind your fucking neck in, prick, before I twist it off!"

An awkward silence fell apart from the post-gig music; you could cut the air with a knife. Tony came out from the bar area. "Okay, lads, that's enough."

Jesse then had a go back. "You kids need to go back and rehearse your entire set; it was a fucking shambles."

Tom, who was also buzzing, launched forward and caught Jesse with a nice right hook, which landed perfectly across his jaw. It sent Jesse sprawling across the floor.

Tony then grabbed Tom and said, "Right, you, out."

Will started complaining to Tony. "Why should Tom be kicked out when that self-obsessed dickhead started the whole thing?"

So Tony turned to them all. "Right, if you lot cannot behave, then you all can fuck off out of my pub. Do I make myself clear"

Daz apologised to Tony. "Sorry, mate, I'm the one who brought these down, so I take full responsibility. They are good lads; they're just a bit excited by it all."

Tony nodded. "Okay, you can all stay, but stay away from each other."

Jesse was still sitting on the floor holding his jaw. He didn't look at anyone. He then got up. "Come on, lads, let's get the fuck outta here." He went up to Tony and held his hand out. "Money." The arrogance was still a problem for this guy, who didn't know when to turn it off.

Even his own band mates just stood there with dirty looks towards their frontman.

Tony then got the money out of his pocket. He went to give it to Jesse but then just let it fall on the floor. Jesse picked up the money and turned around. He walked back to the stage area to pack up his gear, with the others in tow.

Jim said, "We need to go back in there to get our stuff, because he'll probably smash it up."

Tony looked amused at what Jim had said, "Don't worry; he won't do a thing. If they did, they'd get a good kicking from the bouncers and I would take the money back off them." Jim's mind was racing. The anxiety was pushing through again. The drugs he had taken obviously had overridden his medication and he was now a mess. He made his excuses and went outside to get some air. The night was cool. He took a couple of large breaths to try and ease his state. He lit up a smoke and took a walk down the street, looking into all the shops. He took a turn up an alleyway. He just wanted to be alone, as there were still quite a few people on the street. He really needed that time to get himself together.

Jim fell back against a wall. He slid down to his haunches, taking big drags on his cigarette and looking out into the sky.

"Hello, are you all right?"

A voice came from someone at the end of the alleyway. The figure moved up in the darkness towards him and leant against the wall.

"Are you okay?"

Jim just stared up at this girl, her long hair blowing in the slight breeze as she slid down beside him.

"I hope you don't mind, but I followed you from the pub; I saw you playing. I thought you were really good. I can't really say the same for the other band – that singer was too much," she said with a chuckle.

When Jim finally got his bearings, he spoke. "Oh, sorry. Yeah, thank you for that, and no, I don't mind you sitting down. I just needed to get out, get some air."

She smiled. "So what's your name? I'm Katrina."

"I'm Jim. My friends call me Jim. Pleased to meet you, Katrina." Jim stuck out his hand for a handshake and she obliged.

"Likewise. So have you guys been playing long?"

"No, not really. It's only our second gig, but we claim it's our first because the other one was a complete disaster. Oh, and thanks again for liking our band, and yes to what you said about that other band. They were all right guys, except for that singer. Fucking Jesse Knight. I mean, come on, that cannot be his real name. The man was full of shit."

Katrina smiled. "So, are you from around here?"

"Yeah, well, the other side of town. And you?"

"I was a student here, and then I stayed on. I'm from Oxford originally, but I wasn't clever enough to get into the university there, and so I came here."

Jim nodded. His anxiety levels were dropping now, and he needed another beer.

"So do you fancy coming back to the pub with me for a drink, and to meet my idiot friends?" Jim said.

"Yes, that would be nice. Do you have any more cigarettes on you? I had my last one back there."

Jim pulled a couple out and they headed back to the pub.

As they entered, Will shouted over, "Where the fuck have you been?"

Jim explained about needing some air and that his head didn't feel right, and then he introduced Katrina to everyone.

Tom then said, "You wanna watch him, you know, he's a wrongun."

Jim told him to shut up while laughing. Ben then came out from the back. He was a little drunk and stoned. "Hey, Jim, I've just had words with that singer. I told him he was a pretentious wanker."

"Ben, this is Katrina."

"Oh, sorry mate, didn't know you were with a bird."

Katrina just glared at Ben. "I'm no bird, thank you very much."

Ben's girlfriend then punched him in the arm for being so disrespectful and gave him the third degree. She then made her excuses to go to the toilet.

Will, Tom and the others burst out laughing. "Told you, Ben, didn't she?" Tom said.

Ben apologised, and his face went bright red. "Err, anyway, let me get you a drink, as an apology for my comment."

Katrina smiled. "It's okay; James is going to get me one, aren't you, James?"

As she winked at him, Jim blushed. "Yeah, what would you like?"

Will then said, "Oooooooohhh, James, is it now?" in a high-pitched voice.

Jim just stared at him as if to say, "Shut up."

"Vodka orange please." Jim nodded. "And I'll have a pint, thanks."

The night eased on with everyone sitting around, having a laugh.

"Right-oh, people," Ben said over everyone. "I've gotta be off; said I'd go for a few beers with Rob. I hope you don't mind."

They all said it was cool and that they would meet up tomorrow. Ben then made his way over to Daz and Zack for a pick-me-up and they went off to make the deal. Ben turned and said his farewells again and headed out. The rest of them spent the rest of the night in the bar, drinking.

Chapter 9

The next day, Jim looked at his phone. He had three missed calls from Ben's mum, for they all had each of their parents' numbers. Jim then rang back.

A sobbing voice came over the phone. It was Ben's mum.

"Hello, Sue, everything okay?" Jim asked with justified questioning in his voice.

"Hello, Jim, it's … it's Ben. He-he's … DEAD!" She then burst out crying, and then a sound came over like she had dropped the phone. Jim reeled back against the headboard, in that split second trying to figure out if what he just heard was true, or if he had just heard it wrong. There was a silence, then the voice of Ben's dad came on the phone.

"Hello, Jim." His voice was extremely low and sombre.

"Hello, Ray." Jim's voice was frantic. "Did I hear that right? What … What's going on? What's happened?" The panic was setting deep in him. There was a momentary silence.

"Yes, it's true. Erm … we know he came down to see you play and that he went on to a club with his girlfriend (who by then had decided to go home earlier, before the incident) and that Rob."

Rob had explained everything to the police, and the police had relayed what was said to Ben's parents.

There was a long pause. "Hello, Ray?" Jim said, his voice now shaking with the fear of what was going to come. Ben's dad then answered. Jim heard him blow out a deep breath.

"Yes, err, after the club, they started walking to get a taxi. As they did, they were followed by a group of lads who were hurling abuse at them; they obviously wanted trouble. And then they were chased. Rob said they got split up and they went on chasing Ben, as Ben was behind him, and he stated that he heard a loud scream. He said that he turned to see that the lads weren't chasing him any more, so he then ran back to try and find Ben. He was lying on the floor within an alleyway. He noticed the blood flowing from two stab wounds in Ben's stomach; he then called an ambulance." Jim was now tearing up.

"They say he was dead on arrival at the hospital."

Jim now slipped off his bed and onto the floor; his own demons were now racing towards him, just to add another layer of darkness upon him. This was another thing he could not shake on top of this terrible news. Jim then said he was so sorry and could not believe it. They said their goodbyes and hung up. He just sat there, staring at the wall, feeling nothing, hearing no sound. Everything just seemed to have switched off. Life just stood still. A text came through. It was Will, then another from Tom. So Jim guessed that they had just received the news. For Jim didn't open up the texts.

After a while of just sitting there, he forced himself up and went downstairs. A dizzy feeling took over him and it seemed the whole house was spinning. He made his way into the kitchen and looked out of the window. He then threw up in the sink and fell back onto the kitchen table, sending the plates and glasses his mum had just set for breakfast crashing to the floor.

His mum heard the noise and ran into the kitchen to find Jim on the floor, crying.

"Oh my god, Jim, what's wrong!"

Jim started hitting his head with his hand. "Oh fucking hell, why did this happen? WHY!" "What's happened, Jim? What's the matter?" his mum said, with an extremely worried look etched on her face.

"It's Ben. He's ... He's DEAD! HE'S FUCKING DEAD!"

She just stood in shock at what she just heard. "What! How? When?" She rubbed her head in disbelief.

"I just had a call from his parents; they said he was chased when coming out of one the bars in town, him and that fucking Rob!"

"I thought he was with you last night at your gig?"

"He was, but then Ben and his girlfriend went after to meet Rob, as Ben had promised to have a drink with him."

Jim then managed to get himself up. His mum made him a drink. He sat down, and the tears streamed from his eyes. His phone then rang. It was Tom. They spoke about it, both crying, and then Jim called Will to chat about it. Jim made his way back upstairs, took one of his pills but then spat it out; he didn't want to feel good. He felt he didn't deserve it.

He remained in his room until the evening when he decided to just get away.

He texted Daz and asked him where he would be in the next half hour – as usual down the local. Jim then grabbed his acoustic guitar and went downstairs and into the garage where his dad kept all his beer. He put eight cans into a bag and then just left without saying anything.

He got to the pub and saw the two playing pool also as usual. He got himself a double Jack Daniels and downed it, then went over and in low tone said, "All right?" Jim scored a bag of weed. Zack asked him if he was okay. Jim didn't acknowledge him; he just turned and headed back out without saying goodbye.

Daz and Zack just looked at each other. "Fucking hell; what's going on with him?" Daz said. Both shrugged and carried on playing. Jim walked the streets aimlessly in a daze; all those thoughts of Ben just came flooding back into his head, causing him to tear up. His mind was falling due to everything; he needed to just get away from these streets. But it seemed the houses were narrowing in, not letting him get away. Jim made his way to the park and then up to the woods and beyond, over the fields to the canal and river. He found a secluded spot near the river away from prying eyes, opened a can and rolled his first joint, turning his phone off so as not to be disturbed. He lay back into the grass, taking deep drags on his spliff and big swigs on his beer. He grabbed his guitar, just playing anything that came to him. The sky was darkening as the evening fell to the night.

Jim stared deep into the vastness of the night, shouting towards the sky.

"Why him? Why Fucking him!"

He started to cry while strumming his guitar; his mind collected all the thoughts of his friends all together having those laughs. Brightness fell into Jim's mind, which lit up this dark world he was now in. Through all these memories Jim half-cracked a smile. He thought the effects of the dope and booze were now kicking in, sort of comforting him. He opened another can, rolled another joint and dug out his notebook he always kept, for he never knew when these ideas would come. And he just started to write those lyrics for his friend. It was one of the best if not the best song he had ever written. But he wished Ben could be there with him to criticise his song, like he did. His head sank as he thought that those days were now gone.

After he had completed the song, he wrote a few words, which in turn became a poem to his departed friend. He leaned back, resting his head on his bag, staring again deep into the darkening sky. It was a clear night. The stars were staring down like a million cats' eyes keeping watch over him, in his sadness. And as he had done in his back garden, he awoke with the sun blazing down; he felt a dizziness. His back was again wet from the morning dew, the cold lashing around his neck. His throat was dry; he was feeling the effects of the night's consumption. But still the visions of the night never left him. Jim switched his phone back on to see all the missed calls and worrying texts asking where he was and if he was safe, etcetera.

He just looked at them while smoking a cigarette and smiled. He felt sense of calm that there were people looking out for him. A feeling of guilt came over him for thinking that. He shouted an apology to Ben.

"I'm so sorry for thinking that, Ben."

His mind was scrambling for a sense of ease which wouldn't come. He texted his folks saying he was all right and he'd be back soon and not to worry; he just needed some time. And as he lay back down, he remembered it was Monday and he was supposed to be at work.

Jim's panic set in. He immediately rang Terry, for it was his first day and he didn't want to let Terry down. This job meant so much to him. When Terry answered, Jim broke out into his grovelling.

"Hello, Terry, Jim here. I'm so sorry I haven't made it. A good friend was killed over the weekend and I'm just not coping. I don't want to let you down. But if you want to let me go, I'll fully understand." There was a short silence.

"Hello, Jim. Yes, I've heards about whats happened. Your mum called to lets me know and there's no needs for any apologies; it's very understandable. Takes as much time as you needs. Your job will still be here, so you don'ts needs to worry. Oh, and gets yourself home – your folks are worried."

Jim felt a huge relief, but still the panic had set in again. The feeling just kept eating away at him. He thanked Terry for his understanding and said he would be back as soon as possible.

Jim's phone rang; it was his mum. He let it ring off and texted back, again saying he was okay and just needed a little time; he was sorry for all the worry. Texts came in from all his friends. Daz even sent a message asking where he was.

Jim switched his phone off again. He didn't want any more disturbance, but the tears came back. He sat looking over the river, his knees tucked under his chin, rocking back and forth, his mind racing and his body shivering. Squeezing his head, this time the feeling of this great loss was all the more intense. Jim rolled up another joint, putting extra into it to make it that bit stronger, and all the while the black hood emerged, falling deeper into the abyss. He had none of his anti-depressant pills on him, so he thought the self-medication would have to do. But it sent him deeper. He was really thinking about just throwing himself into the river and just being done with it. He lit up his disjointed joint and took huge drags on it. He needed to rid himself of this torture.

As the dope started to take effect, Jim opened another can. They were kept cool by the cold ground. He rubbed his face, ran his hands through his long, greasy hair and leaned back against a tree. He fell back into a deep sleep.

"Jim, Jim. Wake up. Come on, man, wake up."

As Jim awoke, a couple of blurry shapes were leaning over him, and Jim slammed back against the tree.

"What the fuck do you want? Who the fuck are you?"

Tom and Will looked at each other. Jim then got his focus.

"Oh, hello. How did you find me?"

"Well, we figured you'd go somewhere out of the way and this is the most out-of-the-way place around here," Tom said.

Jim smiled. "Yeah, I just couldn't handle it. I just collapsed inside and needed out." Will and Tom sat down.

"Well, I see you've been busy," Will said, looking at all the beer cans, cigarette butts and roaches littering the floor. Jim just stared at the ground, quite embarrassed now.

"Well, I did write a new song and a poem about Ben; you wanna hear it?"

Both nodded. Jim then picked up his guitar and started playing while they both took a couple of cans from the bag, lit cigarettes and listened.

When he had finished, Jim said, "Well, what do you think?"

Tom sniffed and Will turned away as the emotions took hold.

"That was fucking excellent, mate," exclaimed Will with Tom in full agreement.

They sat there talking for a while about everything. Jim brought up the idea that they should go and see Ben's mum and dad. Will said, "I feel it's a bit soon. Leave it a couple of days so they can somehow process the whole situation." All agreed.

They got back to Jim's house late in the afternoon. Jim's mum ran out.

"Oh, Jim, are you okay?" She thanked Will and Tom for finding him and bringing him back.

"I would've come back eventually. There was really no need to send out a search party," Jim said with the usual sarcasm.

His mum said, "I didn't send them – they went themselves."

"Well, okay then. Right, guys, thanks for coming to my rescue and saving me, but I'm just gonna go in now and sleep for a thousand years." He smiled. "Catch you later for a jam, if I wake up."

They all agreed, said their farewells and went. Jim made his way to the shower, switched it on and just stared at himself in the mirror. He looked awful. "Fuck it!"

Chapter 10

The alarm crashed into life. Tuesday morning had arrived. Jim felt an element of calm, like he had cast all those sad emotions out. He sat up and thought about Ben. He dug out his lyrics and the poem he had written and ran through them to see if they still made any sense.

Jim got himself ready and went down to the breakfast table. His dad looked over his paper.

"You okay, Jim?" Jim just nodded and without saying a word drank his tea and grabbed a round of toast.

"Right, I'm off to work. See you later."

"Jim," his mum called after him, "do you think it's a little too soon? Take the rest of the week off; start afresh next week. I'm sure Terry wouldn't mind."

Jim turned back. "No, I've gotta start some time," he said with annoyance in his voice.

He made his way down to the bus stop and lit a cigarette. He stared up and down the street at all the people going about their day, thinking, "Well, Ben's never going see this again," looking at the people, not a smile on anyone's faces, the days rolling into each other, doing the same thing.

"Is he now better off now, away from all this shit? I don't know." He thought he was going crazy with these different thoughts. The bus came down the street past all the local shops and finally pulled up to Jim's stop. He made his way to the back of the bus as it moved on. Jim was thinking, "Is this gonna be my life from now on? This same route forever?"

Sitting at the back of the bus, where there were not that many people, Jim lit up a cigarette. An elderly couple stared back at him with disapproving looks. The elderly man said, "Did you know you're not supposed to smoke on this bus? Can't you read?" He pointed to one of the no smoking signs stuck on the bus window. Jim just smiled and gave the couple a thumbs up.

He then answered back, "No. I can't read. Never made it that far in school," and he gave them a sarcastic smile. The old man turned around while his wife nagged him about how he always had to say something. The bus then went down the high street, towards Jim's stop. Jim then lit up another cigarette and stood waiting for the bus to come to a stop.

The driver looked in his mirror, as he had heard a bit of a commotion; the other passengers were having a go at Jim. He spotted Jim smoking.

"Oi! Put that bleeding thing out! You're not allowed to smoke on here!"

Jim hurried off then turned to the driver. He said, "Well, I'm not on it any more, am I?" and blew a plume of smoke at the driver, making sure all the smoke went in, laughing as he made his way down towards the music shop.

While passing the numerous shops, cafes and offices, especially the offices, Jim looked in at all those people staring blankly into their computers.

Were they really happy with their lives? "No, they can't be," he thought.

As Jim walked into the shop, staring at all the guitars on the wall and all the other instruments, a big smile stretched across his face.

"Happy – are they, fuck. This is true happiness," he thought as Terry then appeared from out the back.

"Hello, Jims. How's it goings? Good to see yous."

He came from behind the counter and shook Jim's hand.

"I'm glad to see you're doings okay. To be honest I didn't thinks you woulds come in this soon."

Jim nodded. "Well, I didn't want to be sat at home all day pondering over what happened. Nothing I can do now, but I needed a little time, you know, to kind of digest the whole situation." Terry said he fully understood.

"Okay, wells, we've got deliveries coming ins, abouts half an hour – you could deal with that. Be a great help."

Terry showed Jim where to put his coat and where the deliveries came in and what to do. "Right, first thing: make a tea. See how you are at that."

Jim smiled. "Oh right. I'm the tea boy now?"

Terry shrugged his shoulders. "Gotta starts somewhere," he said and winked.

While Jim was having his tea and a smoke, chatting to Terry about musical stuff, instruments different bands, etcetera, the delivery lorry came in. Terry spoke to the driver as Jim went to the back when the driver opened the roller door. There was an array of different boxes containing instruments, music books, etcetera. This got Jim very excited.

He began lugging all the stock inside, Terry showing him the ropes, where to take the stuff. All the while Jim was eyeing all the guitars on display. He particularly liked a sparkling burgundy Epiphone SG Special. He loved the shape and everything about it, plus it was more within his price range.

"So, Terry, any chance of a discount on the SG?"

"You's a bit of a cheeky bastard. Justs starting ands already asking for discounts," he said, chuckling.

"Well, the way I see it, you don't ask, you never know."

"Well, we'll see how you go on," Terry said.

"Fair enough."

"I've got to nip outs. Be backs about half an hour. Woulds you be all right workings behind the counter tills I gets back?"

Jim's anxiety kicked in. He was thinking, "Shit, I've gotta run the shop. Say I fuck up?"

Jim took a deep breath and puffed out his cheeks with the exhale.

"Yeah, that'll be fine," he said, rubbing his head, raising his eyebrows.

Just before Terry left, he showed Jim how to work the till. "Right, here's how to work the till."

Running through the workings, Jim was in a deep panic. But he didn't want to alarm Terry with his worries so he just said, "Yep, that'll be ok, I've got it."

"Anythings yous is unsure ofs, just let the customer knows I'll be backs in a bit."

Jim thought Terry's speech impediment was getting worse. He had at first found it funny but now it was starting to get on his nerves.

"Rights then, I'ms off."

Jim stood there, behind the counter, feeling really uncomfortable, when the first of the customers started coming in. Sweat started to pour down his back; his hands became clammy. "Excuse me, would it be okay if I tried this guitar?"

Jim went over and sorted the guy out by tuning the guitar and grabbing him a stool.

"If you need anything else, just give me a shout."

Another customer was waiting to buy some strings. More nerves kicked in, and so in his panic Jim got the wrong strings down, then also messed up the till. It was now crisis mode. He was screaming inside, "You stupid fucking idiot – what are you doing?" Self-doubt was flowing through him like the blood in his veins.

"Are you okay, mate?" the guy getting the strings said. "You look a bit stressed."

Jim just stared at him, scratching his head.

"Yeah, I take it it shows. My first day and the owner had to go out, so I am a bit panicked."

The customer showed sympathy for Jim. "It's okay, mate. Take all the time you need; just don't fuck up my change," he said, smiling. This was the icebreaker; it took all the panic away. From then on, Jim took the reins and went with it, his confidence growing with each customer.

He was now happy. Then in came a guy who was mainly looking at all the electric guitars.

He made his way over to the counter.

"Hello, not seen you in here before. Take it you're a new starter?"

Jim replied, "Yep, first day."

"Okay, well, is Terry about? I usually deal with Tel; he knows exactly what I want, and you being new and all."

Jim automatically took an instant dislike to the man. "Well, Terry had to go out, so he left me to handle things."

The man looked at Jim in a sheepish way.

"Well, I'll wait till he gets back. Like I said, I usually deal with Terry personally."

Jim shrugged his shoulders and said, "Fair enough," and went about serving other customers.

The man. again approached Jim. "You do understand that since you are new here I don't want any mistakes with what I want?"

Jim now was getting quite aggrieved with this guy.

Again Jim said, "That's fair enough; whatever you want; it's fine."

Jim knew he was trying to wind him up, but he held his nerve.

"Do you know how long he'll be?" said the man.

"Be around half an hourish, I guess."

The man was pacing around, getting quite agitated. "I haven't got time for this. Okay, you'll have to do," he said, the arrogance spewing from his mouth.

Jim then turned around. "What do you mean, I'll have to do? Who the fuck do you think you are, talking to me like that!" Jim was now seething.

Then came the killer line. "Do you know who I am!"

Jim stood there in amazement and started laughing. The other customers looked at this guy, shaking their heads, also sniggering at the arrogance.

Jim then said, "Oh yeah, I know who you are."

And the guy said, "You do?" sounding quite surprised.

"Yeah, you are a massive arrogant twat, who thinks he's somebody." Jim then questioned the other customers, asking them if they knew who he was.

Each of them shook their heads, murmuring, "No idea" and "Who is he?" The guy's face went bright red from anger and also embarrassment.

"I'm Roger Nolan. I was in the Hundred Feet Stare, and we had a hit in the sixties in the charts." Still, no one had an inkling who he was.

Jim said, "No idea, mate. Anyway, do you want what you came in for or not, cause there's other people waiting."

He then relented. "Okay, I'll have four packs of D'Addario acoustic strings elevens and four packs of Ernie Balls electric elevens."

"Is that everything?" said Jim.

Roger nodded. Jim then went to get the strings and rang up the total. Roger said, "All that for eight packs of strings? I can get them cheaper across town."

Jim said, "Well, go there then if you're not happy. Also, you wanna learn to control yourself, mate, and stop with this big 'I am' attitude. You do not impress anyone."

Roger snatched the bag out of Jim's hand and went to walk out just as Terry was walking in. "Hello, Roger, how's are you?" Terry said.

Jim saw that Terry was being told about everything that had happened, and that if he didn't fire him, Roger would take his business elsewhere.

He saw Terry frown. "Nows holds on, Roger. He's new, first days, no needs to give him a hard time."

Jim then shouted over, "Oh yeah, he also gave me the 'do you know who I am' speech."

The other customers in the shop were listening in and laughing at what Jim had just said. Terry said, "Oh Roger, yours still not goings with the 'do you knows who I am' things again." Terry was shaking his head and a big smirk was etched across his face.

"You have gottas lets that go. No one knows whos you are nowsadays."

Roger then turned to Jim. "Next time I come back and he's still here, that's it, Terry, my business is going with me."

"Whats ever you says, mate," said Terry and opened the door for him to leave.

Terry walked over to the counter and gut the stuff down he had gone out to buy. "Well, I sees you've mets Roger. He's a bit of a bighead. He's once had a minor hit in the sixties and he's played on it ever since. He can be quite embarrassing, especially when he's had a few."

Jim shook his head. "You say a BIT of a bighead."

That evening Jim texted to cancel the rehearsal. He wasn't feeling it after the day's excitement. He called up Katrina and met up with her for a drink and explained all the drama that had unfolded during the day.

"Wow, and on your first day. Talk about being thrown in at the deep end."

Jim sat there, nodding. "Yep, pretty crazy." By then, Jim had started to zone out, drifting off. His hands started to shake. A single tear streamed down his face.

"Are you all right, Jim?" A concerned tone rang through her question. She asked him about the medication and whether he was taking it regularly.

His reply was, "Not as often as I should."

Jim shook his head. "I just don't feel right within myself." His panic was again setting in. "Shit shit shit!" Jim said while hitting the side of head. "I can't feel right; I never feel right."

Katrina then leaned over and hugged him. "Come on, let's go."

They headed back to her flat, which was located just outside town so not far to walk.

When they arrived, a car was parked outside. "Hello, Katrina." Katrina looked round.

"Oh fuck, it's my ex." She went over to the car. "Yes, what do you want?"

Jim sat on the wall looking on; he heard talking but couldn't make out what was being said. Katrina came walking back over. "Come on, Jim, let's go inside."

The car door was flung open and a small, stocky guy got out. "Oh, so you're the new guy."

Jim's anxiety levels grew. He started to shake uncontrollably; he knew what was coming.

As the man approached, there was a smile streaming across his face and not a friendly one at that.

"Hello, mate. So I guess you're the new one," he said again. "Well, did you know we're still together?"

Katrina shouted back, "No we're fucking not!" She dragged Jim off the wall, by which time her ex had got Jim by the other arm.

"I just want to talk to the new boy."

Jim then pushed him away. "Look, why don't you just fuck right off? You ain't together any more, so fucking do one."

A swinging punch came around and struck Jim in the side of the face, throwing him against the wall. A foot then came into the side of his ribs. Jim was now pretty winded, crouching in a defensive position while more blows came raining down. Katrina was shouting at her ex to leave Jim alone, grabbing on his jacket.

Jim, while down, managed to compose himself and flung himself at the other guy. He pushed him against the opposite wall, laying blows to his face, head and everywhere. The fight then went to the floor, each of them inflicting more punches on one another. Katrina was shouting for them to stop. A couple of blokes who were walking past saw what was going on and went over to break it up. "Come on now, leave it!" they shouted while pulling them apart.

Katrina again grabbed Jim. "Come on, Jim, let's go, and you, fuck off. Come round here again, Joe, and I'm calling the police!"

One of the men who broke up the fight said, "You heard her – fuck off."

Joe got back in his car and sped off. Once inside, Katrina got some water and a towel and started wiping the blood from Jim's nose.

"I'm so sorry, Jim, I didn't realise he was gonna turn up." She kissed Jim, running her hands through his hair.

"It's okay. Typical jealous boyfriend scenario." Jim cracked a smile. "Well, we're just gonna mark this down as a shit day, and that also your ex is called Joe," he said while rolling up a spliff. "How I need this."

Katrina smiled, grabbing his hand. "Come on, let's go to bed."

The next morning, Jim went to the bathroom and looked in the mirror. He had a slight black eye and a few bruises around his cheekbone.

"Well, you've seen better days," he said to himself.

As he got back in bed, Katrina was now awake, "Good morning. How are feeling?" she asked.

"Well, not that bad really, except for the black eye, bruises and sore ribs," Jim said while lying back on the pillow. "I wonder what all the customers are gonna say when they see me," he said, smiling. Katrina gave him a hug.

"Do you want me to come with you to explain" She felt an ultimate amount of responsibility.

"No, it's okay, it will be fine. I'll tell Terry and everyone I fell or had a fight with a door." A sarcastic grin was etched across Jim' face. Katrina went to the kitchen to get Jim some breakfast and make him a pack up for- his lunch.

"Here you go, get this down you."

"Wow, breakfast in bed; I am being spoilt."

After his breakfast, Jim lay back, staring at the ceiling.

"Do you think we'll make it – the band, I mean." Jim's voice echoed with doubt. "Sometimes I feel I'm not worth anything, that I won't achieve anything good in my life."

Katrina looked up at him. "Well, you have me," she said jokingly.

"No, I'm serious. I've never felt I was worth anything and that music and writing is all I have, what I enjoy. So if that fails, then I feel I won't have achieved anything I really want."

"Look, if you want something so bad then you just have to go for it and keep going and never give up, then one day things will happen."

"Yeah, I suppose. I'm just sick of all my negative thoughts and the shit that runs through my head."

"Right, anyway, you better get up or you'll be late for work. I'll drop you off."

Jim thanked her for being there for him.

Chapter 11

When Jim arrived at the shop, the delivery van was pulling in. He got to work helping unload the stock. Terry came out.

"Mornings, how's are you doing todays?"

Jim then turned around. "Morning, Terry, just getting the stuff in."

When Terry saw Jim's face, he said, "My god, what's happened to yous?"

Jim smiled.

"Well, I had a fight with a door and it won."

Terry went over and had a look.

"Likely story; whose yous had a fight with?"

Jim looked very sheepish as he moved away. Panic set in. He was worried for his job if he explained about the previous evening. After everything was unloaded, Jim went about his duties with all the new stock and rearranging the window display, etcetera. While the shop was quiet, Terry came out with some coffees, "Jim, that's all right for a minute. Comes and sits down and haves a drink."

Jim went over grabbed his drink. "Okay if I go for a smoke?"

"Sure, I'lls comes out with yous."

Jim knew he was going to be questioned about his face, so he just sat looking at the people in the offices which overlooked the rear yard of the shop, rows of robotic people staring blankly into those computer screens that were reflecting off the glass. Terry sat down. "You gots another one?" he said nodding towards Jim's cigarettes.

Jim pulled one out. "Here you go."

Jim was still staring out at the office block.

"Do you think they are really happy, stuck in the confines of those office spaces?" he questioned Terry, trying to deflect from being questioned about his face.

Terry pondered the thought. "Well, I suppose somes of them must, and again others must hate it, likes any other job."

"It would do my fucking head in being stuck in there, surrounded everyday by all those people. It would feel to me like the walls were be closing in, and you have to just sit there and take it," Jim said with a contemptuous tone in his voice.

"Wells, it appears to me that's yous have thought alots about those individuals in those offices, but just remember one thing. You are not there, so don't let it bother you."

"Doesn't bother me; I just thought about it."

Terry drew on his cigarette. "Now's, young Jim, yous gonna tell me about these bruises on your face, and don't give that 'a door hit me' bullshit. You thinks I was born yesterday?"

So Jim explained all about the previous evening's entertainment.

"I knews it," Terry said, stubbing out his cigarette. "So the jealous boyfriend scenario; we'ves all beens there."

Jim looked quite relieved. "I thought you were gonna sack me for coming in like this. You know how it will look to all the customers."

No, I'm a man ofs the world. I knows shit happens when yous least expect it; sometimes it's just the ways it is."

The sound of the front door alarm went off.

"Right, break over, and remembers, anything yous want to talk about, no matter how's difficult, you can always comes to me." Jim thanked Terry and went back inside.

The rest of the day went without any more drama, just Terry every now and again winding Jim up about his face and re-arranging the rehearsal for that evening. They had all assembled in the garage for a jam when Tom spoke up as Jim entered the garage.

"Fuck me, what happened to you?"

Will then took a look at Jim's face. "Ooooh yer, that looks nasty. What happened?"

So Jim had to troll through the previous night's entertainment, with a slight amount of sympathy and a shitload of piss-taking. Jim then broke the constant torment, saying about trying to get a proper rehearsal room.

"I really think it's time we get down to a real rehearsal room. I mean, in here is okay but quite limited with volume and that. At least we can make whatever noise we want in a proper place."

All were in an agreement. So after the rehearsal, Jim went on his phone to look for a proper rehearsal studio.

"Well, I could've looked on the shop noticeboard. Loads of people bring in things like that – oh well," Jim said as he was scrolling through his phone.

He then found one. "Agh, here we go. I've heard about this place; it's uptown. Sound studios, rehearsal rooms and recording studio."

"That's the place with rooms in the cellar bit," Will said.

"Well, it's a bit bigger than a cellar; I've heard it's massive under there," Tom said.

"Okay, I'll give them a call now. It looks like they're still open." Jim checked on the website for the details. As Jim called the studio, Tom and Will broke out the smokes, playing around with their instruments. Jim said, "Will you guys shut the fuck up; I can't hear myself," just as the guy answered. "Oh sorry, mate."

Jim then asked about studio availability times and prices. He was told it was fifteen pounds an hour and available at six p.m. on Thursday. Jim told the guy that that would be cool, and they would see him then. "Well, that's sorted."

"Oh, Jim you better sort your face before we play again," Tom said, smirking.

Will's mouth twisted into a smile before he burst out laughing.

That night when Jim got home, he started feeling very strange. The anxiety came on and off. One minute he was okay then the next he was not, and a strange whirring sound moved through his head. He couldn't figure out what was going on. Jim told his mum, and she asked him if he had been taking his pills regularly. Jim said he hadn't.

"Well, I think you better start taking them at regular times. It's probably not taking them that's affecting you."

So Jim took a couple just to get them into his system. He took his acoustic out, trying to write some new material, when his phone went. It was Ben's dad, informing him of the date of the funeral. "Hello, Jim, I'm just calling to let you know the funeral will held the weekend after next."

Jim froze as he was being told. He was just getting himself together, more or less, but now those images of his friend came flooding back. He thanked him for letting him know and said that he would tell the others, to save him calling. Ben's dad also thanked Jim for doing that. As those tears came again, Jim proceeded to call Will and Tom plus other friends who had known Ben. That night as he was just drifting off, his eyes fading into the realm of sleep, Jim felt his duvet being pulled away from him. The temperature of the room seem to plummet to freezing. He shivered as he tried to pull the duvet back but still it was being pulled away. "Fuck's sake, who's that? Mum, dad, pack it in, it's freezing in here!"

He then heard his name being called in a familiar voice. Jim was still halfway between being awake and asleep when he heard it again.

"Jim, mate, wake up, it's me, Ben."

Jim froze. He opened his eyes, and through the darkness and his bleary eyes he could see the cold on his breath. A figure sat at the end of his bed. He opened his eyes wider and the figure moved forward. "Hello, Jim." He was now face to face with his dead friend.

Jim screamed. He sprang up, breathing heavily, and looked around. No one was there.

"What the fuck was that!" he said.

Disorientated, he leaned back against the headboard, still looking around. Sweat was pouring down his face and his heart was racing. Jim got up, went to the bathroom and washed his face. He looked at himself in the mirror.

"Am I going fucking insane?" he kept splashing water over his face and neck.

"Gotta be the effects of this medication," he thought. The next morning, the heavy sound of his alarm rang out. Jim woke up. He was still in that confused state from the previous night, thinking he must have dreamt the whole thing, and how could it be real. But it had seemed so real at the time.

While at breakfast, Jim got a call from Tony, the manager at the Phoenix, about a gig that weekend – another support slot.

"Yes, definitely," Jim said. That seemed to make him forget for the time being about the previous night. Straight away he called the others about the gig. All were pretty excited. Tom said, "I hope we don't get another dickhead band like the other one."

That day at work, Jim let Terry know about the gig at the weekend.

"Well, I'll trys and gets down. Be goods to sees you guys play." Jim was happy to see that Terry had an interest in what he was doing, since his parents never really showed much. Jim was busy with some customers when Katrina stopped in, as it was near dinner time. "Hello, Jim. I thought you might like to go for dinner."

"Yeah, I'll be with you in a bit."

Katrina looked at him. "I'll be with you in a bit!" The annoyance was deafening.

Terry sat there. He looked over at Jim and shook his head, inhaling loudly as if to say, "You shouldn't have said that."

Jim turned to Terry. "What?"

"Nothing, Jim, but don't be surprised if you get a clout round the ear for saying that. It's like telling a woman to calms down; you just don'ts do it," Terry said sarcastically, still shaking his head and laughing. Luckily for the both of them, Katrina was over by the guitars having a look. Otherwise they'd have both gotten a smack.

She then approached the counter. "Right are you ready, dickhead?"

Jim, just putting his coat on, stopped. "Dickhead?"

"Yep."

Terry stood up. "Oh, I take it I'll see you at the gig on Saturday?"

Katrina glared at Jim. "Oh, the gig that I was not informed about!"

It was clear to Terry that Jim had forgotten to let Katrina know about the weekend's activities by the tone of her voice and the raised eyebrows.

"Oh dear," said Terry, patting Jim on the shoulder and making his way into the back for his dinner. The silent treatment was on all the way to café, while Jim was grovelling and apologising about not telling Katrina about the weekend and that he was only asked that morning to play. Katrina then turned round and said, "I was gonna buy lunch for you. Now you can forget it; you can pay."

Jim agreed. "Am I forgiven now?"

"Nope."

After lunch, Jim said, "See you later," and gave Katrina a peck on the cheek.

"Possibly", she said, as she started to walk away. Jim then got down on his knees in the middle of the pavement.

"Oh, Katrina, please don't leave me this way, I'm soooo sorry." He had his hands clasped together as though he were praying, feigning a cry.

Katrina stopped and looked back, shaking her head. "Get up, you idiot." She smiled and blew him a kiss. "Okay. I'll see you later."

Jim, still on his knees, said, "Oh thank you, my sweetheart, thank you," while passers-by just looked at him, shaking their heads. Back at the shop, Terry was serving some customers.

"Agh, so you're still alive then?"

"Yep; just gave her the 'who wears the trousers in this relationship' speech, and that was that."

Terry laughed. "Yeah, right."

"It's true," Jim said.

Terry blew out his cheeks. "Okay, if you like."

Jim just grinned and went about his duties.

Chapter 12

That evening, Jim got together all the songs for the rehearsal for the next day, picking up his guitar going through some of them, as he liked running through to see if he could add anything else to make them sound better. Jim's phone text alarm went off. It was Tom. Tom said he was going down the pub. Jim agreed to go, as he hadn't been down with his mates for a while since being with Katrina. He said he would meet Tom down there. Jim carried on sorting the set list out and was surprised at how many songs they had – more than enough for an album. Jim felt really excited. He got down the pub around eight. He saw Daz and Zack as usual on the pool table doing a new way of dealing from under the cushion on the corner seat by the side of the pool table: drugs under the seat cushion; customer sits down and places money under the cushion while swiping the drugs. All very strategic, that's if you were trained by an inept strategist. For it was plain to see what was going on.

But Jim would be over there shortly to do exactly the same thing.

"Hello, boyz," Jim said while approaching the bar. The greeting was acknowledged in the same manner. Jim had walked into the middle of a conversation they were having about the racing Will and Tom had put bets on that afternoon. Jim interrupted.

"So, lads, I've got the songs all sorted out for the rehearsal tomorrow. Looking forward to it? Oh, well, don't sound too excited," Jim said while grabbing his pint. "Right, I'm just gonna go and get something to cheer me up since you two are bundle of laughs."

Jim went over to Daz and Zack. Jim stood about three feet away from the pool table. "Knock, knock," Jim said.

Zack said, "You really are a sarcastic twat, aren't you," while smirking.

"Well, this is your office, isn't it? I tell you what, if anybody wanted to find you, they wouldn't have to look very hard."

"Who would want to find us, apart from customers?" Zack said.

Jim looked at him, quite amused. "Well, I don't know, police maybe? Rival dealers?" Jim said, shrugging his shoulders.

Daz frowned. "We run this fucking manor. Anybody tries to step in," he made his hand into a gun shape, "Bang."

Daz then said "Have not seen you around in a while – you blanking us with that bird?"

"Katrina, you mean," Jim said, quite annoyed.

Both of them said, "Ooooooooohhh," in unison. "Touched a nerve there, didn't we," both said, laughing.

"No!"

Daz then put his cue down. "Jimmy, my boy, I've got something here that will make us friends again."

He pulled Jim aside and pulled out a bag of coke. "So, you up for it?"

Jim stared at the bag. "Is that what I think it is?"

"Yep, it is."

Jim's eyes lit up. "Yep, definitely."

So Jim followed Daz to the toilets, where he lined up four rows of coke on the sink. Daz went first, snorting up two lines.

"Whoooh, fuck me!" he said as the effect of the drug took hold. Then Jim took the rolled-up a ten-pound note and snorted the rest. He fell back against the wall, pupils dilated. A rush flowed through Jim's entire being.

"Wow!" Jim said, "If there's a heaven then this must be the feeling you get."

Daz laughed. "Yep, definitely. and there's plenty more where that came from," he said while pulling another smaller bag of coke out of his pocket, which he placed in Jim's coat.

"That's another little freebie, since you are a loyal customer."

"Well, I will be back for more of that," Jim said, deeply impressed with it while scoring some more weed and a couple of grams of speed.

Back at the bar, Will and Tom were still sitting there talking the same shit they had been talking when Jim had first arrived.

"Blimey, are you still talking about the fucking racing?"

Tom looked at him. "Wow, you look a bit flushed; what the fuck did Daz do to you in there?" he said and Will burst out laughing.

"Well, just had me a bit of coke. Fuck me – amazing!"

"Jim, why you getting all caught up in that shit? I mean, having a smoke and a bit of speed now and again, that's fair enough, but fucking hell, man, coke? Don't get involved." Tom's concerned voice was full of disapproval.

And Will seconded the motion. "Okay, Jim, you've tried it, now leave it alone. With the state of your mind as it is, that shit's really gonna mess with your head."

Jim then produced the bag out of his pocket. "Well, I got this as another freebie. You sure you don't want to try some?"

Will and Tom just looked at each other. "Agh, fuck it," Will said, "just this once." Tom also caved in. They adjourned to the toilets and Jim laid out a few lines and they proceeded to snort it.

Both Will and Tom said, "Wow, that's fucking amazing!"

Jim laughed. "Told you so."

Back at the bar, while they were ordering more drinks, Daz and Zack came over. "All right, lads, so did Jim tell you about it then?"

Jim just laughed and said, "Yeah, well, at first they were all against it until we had a little session with the stuff you gave me." Both Will and Tom nodded, still playing with their noses, looking all glazed.

"Anyway," Jim again spoke up, "I just want to raise a glass to Ben. I don't feel we've had a proper session in his name." Jim raised his glass. "Here's to Ben, wherever he maybe. Rest easy, mate."

They all joined in the toast, with a few more drinks on top.

Daz then got a phone call. "Right. be there in about ten minutes."

Zack asked, "Have we got to meet them now?"

Daz said, "Yep. Right, lads, it's been entertaining but we've just gotta go and do a bit business."

Jim then said, "Oh yeah? What sort of business?"

"The sort of business I just sorted you out with," Daz said with a grin.

"Well, I'm calling it a night," Will said. "Got to be up at stupid o'clock."

Tom was in agreement but Jim wanted to stay just a little while longer.

"Just gonna stay here a while; got a few things on my mind. Catch you two tomorrow down the studio."

Tom said, "All right, mate, but don't stay too long; you'll never get up."

Will and Tom patted Jim on the back, as they knew he was thinking about Ben. They were all upset about his passing, like Jim, but Jim's fragile state of mind led him to think more about it and it weighed very heavy on him, especially after consuming those drinks and that coke. They were now sending his mind through the roof. Jim did get quite sombre on alcohol without anything on top.

Daz and Zack reached the pub. They stepped inside and ordered a couple of drinks and spotted one of the guys who worked for the main drug supplier they were to have the meeting with.

Daz went over. "Hello, mate, how you doing?" He reached out his hand, but the other guy just looked at him, never raising a smile and not acknowledging the handshake.

Daz said, "Right, suit yourself. Well, could you let us know where the meeting is being held?" Daz was his usual cock-sure self with a sarcastic tone in his voice.

The man raised his eyes as if to say, "Upstairs".

"Much obliged," Daz said, tipping his invisible hat.

Zack took the sign that the man didn't want to be disturbed and left him alone. He didn't want any trouble if they could help it, because these people were not ones to fuck around with. They were a fully tooled up drug gang. As they went up, there were more people standing along the corridor. They were look-outs; Daz and Zack thought the guy at the bar must be the first spotter. Entering the room, they saw a few people whom they knew, rival dealers, etcetera. They all shook hands. They made it a bit of a peace summit between them, because out on the street there was no love lost.

As they all sat down, the main guy stood up and welcomed everyone and introduced himself as Derrick English. He was well known around the criminal fraternity. He was a short thin-ish man in his late sixties with receding grey hair. He didn't seem much to look at, but he had a nasty reputation, plus he had the backup. His men were loyal and didn't take any shit. If you needed to pay, then you paid, simple as.

"Right, I'll just get to it. We have a lot stuff coming through our way. And I want to distribute it between all of you. I'm gonna be the centre of all this. So basically, you'll put my stuff out there, you'll get your perks, but I want kickbacks every two weeks. I'll let you know where and when. You can find me or I'll find you – either way works for me. But fuck me about, and you'll have severe consequences heading your way. Are we understood?"

A murmuring of "Yes" rang round the room.

"Right; we'll talk to you individually and work out a drop off which suits both parties."

As Derrick talked about the distribution, Daz was getting quite aggrieved with what he would call, "This old man's bollocks."

He stared round the room at everyone.

"Why the fuck should I kick my money up to him? A changing of the guard is what's needed." All these thoughts were racing round his head while Zack just sat there, quiet and listening. He wasn't your typical violent drug dealer but would do what was necessary for the job in hand, but for the time being he sat there and just took it all in.

When all was done, Daz stood and said to Zack, "I'm just gonna go and talk to Mr Big." His arrogance was shining through. Zack held back. He didn't want any chitchat; he just wanted what they were getting and just get out.

After all was said and done, Daz and Zack walked out with smiles from ear to ear.

"Fuck me, we're gonna make a killing," Zack said.

Daz then turned to his partner. "Look, you see all those in there? Most are just kids out to make a name by being associated with that old twat, but I've got bigger plans."

Zack said with a lot of apprehension, "What are you talking about? You're not getting one of your stupid ideas, are you?"

Daz smiled. "Come on, trust me, we need to get in the big time where the serious money is, not fucking around at the pub, a bit here, a bit there."

"Okay, what do you have in mind? But the way you're talking doesn't fill me with any confidence."

When they reached their car, Daz laid out his plan. "I think we're more than capable of ripping these guys off and creating our own little firm."

"So let me get this straight. You wanna take Dez English and his crew. You're talking a power grab." Daz lit a cigarette and a huge grin spread across his face as he nodded at the question.

"Have you taken leave of your senses? You must be fucking insane to think that let alone to do it. We'd be fucking dead before we got one foot in the door."

"Come on; we could get enough people on board with this. All we have to do is just make the move – rip off the first drop. Send a message of sorts."

Zack was still unconvinced. But he thought about it. He knew they could get the muscle and the artillery. But this was a massive undertaking. He also knew that Daz wanted to move up the chain. And to do that you really did need to challenge the people already on the scene.

"I'd have to seriously think about it," Zack said. It seemed he was somehow warming to the idea.

Chapter 13

Jim awoke the next morning before his alarm, feeling okay. He sat there thinking about the day ahead and the rehearsal later. A huge smile swept across his face. He leaned over to his drawer, pulled out his medication and popped one. He was going to try and sort himself out and get on top of it. An air of positivity overcame him. He felt strange, since this was a rare occasion. That day at work, Terry came over to him while he was lugging some of the amps from the back of the shop for the window display.

"Jim, I've's got something to tell you. I've gots this friend down in London. Names is Charlie. He's a bit ofs a promoter ands I've's told him about yous. Well, he's coming up at the weekend to watch yous. I hope you don't mind."

Jim nearly dropped the amp he was holding.

"Really?" said Jim. Terry nodded. "Wow, that's brilliant. Thanks, Terry, from me and the boys. We really appreciate it. We have a rehearsal later. I'll let the lads know."

Terry said, "My pleasures. I just hope yous do a bang-up jobs for him, cause yous never knows," and he went back to the counter, as a few customers were lining up. That evening Jim met everyone down at the studio, ready for their first jam in a proper studio.

"All right, lads," Jim said, getting out of his dad's car. He turned to his dad, saying that he'd see him later and thanked him for the lift. When they went in, they were met by a long hallway lined with old mic stands and some cables and leads strewn over hooks on the walls plus a few old amps with bits of tatty carpet left on the top of them. The smell was pretty rank – quite musty and damp. At the end of the hall was a reception area with a glass counter with items for sale underneath – guitar strings, mics, plus a couple of harmonicas for sale. Tom knocked on the counter.

"Hello? Anybody there?" A small, chubby guy walked out. He had long but receding ginger hair and looked to be in his mid- to late fifties.

"Hello, guys, I guess you are here for a studio?" he said while looking through the diary he used for booking in bands. "Yes, you must be Blue Veil Rain. I have Jim down as the contact name," he said. Jim stepped forward. "Yep, that's me. I'm the one you spoke to on the phone."

"Right-oh. You're in room four, just down the hall," he said, pointing the way.

"Thanks a lot," Jim said.

When they got inside, the smell was more potent in there.

"Fuck me, it stinks in here," Tom said, wincing but also laughing.

"Right, let's see what's what," Jim said, scoping the amps and where he was going to go.

Tom said, "Well, I guess I'll be here," sitting on the drum stool.

Will walked over to a bass amp in the corner of the room, took out his bass and plugged it into the amp. He went to switch it on but nothing came out.

"What the fuck? Piece of shit amp don't work." Jim went over and tried switching it on, but still it was dead.

"Oh, well, that's just great," Jim said, with Will in full agreement. They were voicing their frustration and slagging off the studio, calling the guy who ran it "a fucking prick" and saying, "Stuff don't work," etcetera. Tom leaned back and peered behind the amp and just burst out laughing.

Will looked over to Tom. "What the fuck are you laughing at!"

Jim, also puzzled, shrugged his shoulders. "Yeah, what?"

"You two are a real couple of clowns," Tom said, shaking his head. "Have you looked behind the amp to see why it's not working?"

Will went to the back and looked it over. "No, what? I can't see why."

Tom stood up and went over. He crouched down and picked up the plug and showed it to Will and Jim. With raised eyebrows he said, "You need to plug the fucking thing in first, you tit, and then guess what? Electricity magically appears in the thing you want use."

The sarcasm cut Will deep, and he went bright red. Jim shook his head while face-planting himself.

"Oh, fuck it," Will said.

After that sudden mishap and an introduction on how to use a plug, they got on with jamming, rolling through the numbers for the gig.

Later that evening Jim met Katrina for a drink, telling her about the rehearsal and how much the studio smelled. She wasn't overly impressed. After, they walked down through the town, window-shopping along the closed stores. Jim felt so sorry for the people sleeping in the doorways, as it was not the warmest of nights. One guy was sitting playing an acoustic guitar in a sleeping bag, a small black-and-white dog by his side. Jim went over to give him a bit of change. Instead he pulled a brand-new fiver and handed it to the man. He said, "Go and get something to eat for you and your dog."

The man thanked Jim and told him he would. Jim asked the dog's name and how old it was. The man said the dog's name was Patch (I guess due to its black patches). He said it was an old dog, twelve years old and that it was the only real companion he had apart from his guitar. Jim told him about the gig at the Phoenix that Saturday and that he should come down. Even though it was a pay-to-enter gig, Jim would sort him out.

"Thanks a lot. Oh, what about my dog? I can't leave him outside by himself."

Jim smiled. "No worries. Bring him in with you; we'll sort him a bowl of water and biscuits. Oh, by the way, what's your name?"

"I'm Keith, and you've already met Patch."

"Right-oh, Keith. I'm Jim and this is Katrina."

"You two look very nice, very suited."

Both Jim and Katrina smiled and thanked him. "Right, Keith, we'll see you Saturday, and you, Patch," Jim said while stroking Patch's head.

As they went on, Jim pondered on Keith's situation, on how bad he felt for him and his dog. Katrina agreed but told Jim that what he did was very nice of him. But deep inside she felt unsure about giving the guy money, because she had heard stories about how the homeless could squander it on things other than food, but she kept her feelings to herself and gave him a kiss. She felt bad about having those kinds of feelings, as they were not all like that. She saw the humanity in Jim. Even with all his personal problems, he still had compassion for his fellow man, whom he saw struggling. Jim texted Daz to ask him where he would be in about an hour, as he wanted some more gear, and was he was cool for the stuff – in other words, good for the drugs Jim wanted.

Daz replied that everything was all good and that he would be at the usual spot.

Jim and Katrina made their way down to the pub. Jim wanted some more speed and a bag of weed. Jim now was taking speed more often than not. But he didn't let on to the others that he was. His mind was being pushed moreover with his drug use, even though he was taking his meds. They were becoming more ineffective with his increased intake of speed. They stood at the bar and Jim was feeling anxious. He couldn't keep still. His head kept darting round the room.

"Are you all right, Jim?" Katrina said.

"Yeah, I just feel a little out of sorts."

After getting their drinks, Jim made his excuses to go and talk to Daz and Zack, who were, as they had said, in their usual place at the pool table. Katrina didn't look too happy and blew her cheeks out.

"All right, lads," Jim said, trying to keep his twitching to a minimum. "I just need a bag of that crazy fucking skunk we had the other day (the sort Ben had brought down before their WMC gig) and, say, five grams." of speed

Jim and co were now smoking this new skunk weed, which, as they said, "sent them out in-to the stratosphere".

They made the deal. Daz then went on to tell Jim about the meeting they had had across town, and how they were getting some great contacts and business was going to be booming.

"Very nice. So how about all the other dealers? Are you going to take their patches and claim more business, since you now have the backing?" Jim questioned.

"Well, we've had a sort of truce with all the other dealers, kind of a come together. They figured we would all make more money working together than fighting each other for any sort of control," Zack said. Jim nodded. "Makes sense. Anyway, gotta go. The Mrs is over there; she'll be wondering what I'm up to, so I will catch you later."

Jim made his way back to Katrina. "You okay?" Jim said, looking quite sheepish.

"Yeah, not bad, although I don't like being stuck on my own while you go and score your weed."

"Sorry. It is good weed though. Come on, let's go out back and get one going."

Katrina reluctantly agreed, She really didn't like Jim taking drugs because of how he was. But she didn't own him. So she let him crack on. Also, she smoked a bit, like his friends. A sense of hypocrisy flowed within them all. Jim led the way into the beer garden. He found a table at the bottom, sat down and rolled up the first one. He took four or five hits on it and it kicked in straight away. He passed it over to Katrina and she smoked it and sat back, staring into the sky as the hit took over.

"Wow, that's awesome." she said, her voice a bit croaky.

Jim smiled while he had his drink. Jim then asked if Katrina wanted another drink and said he would get some crisps for the munchies which would inevitably come on. Katrina just smiled and nodded. It was all she could do, for when she tried to speak her lips moved but nothing came out. Jim found it hilarious. He went first to the toilet and into one of the cubicles. He emptied one of the wraps of speed on the back of the toilet, separated it into two lines with his bank card then rolled up a ten-pound note and proceeded to snort it. He could taste the sourness in the back of his throat, which made him gag. After, he went back to the bar to get the drinks and crisps. As he was waiting, he saw a couple of guys sitting at the table talking to Katrina. He got the drinks and went out.

"What's going on here then?" Jim asked, feeling quite annoyed. His paranoia was kicking in.

"Agh, Jim, these are just two nice guys who came over to see why I was sitting by myself," Katrina said, laughing. The two guys sitting with her also laughed and one of them said, "Why would you leave a beautiful lady sitting here by herself? Anybody could whisk her away."

The guy looked at Jim and winked. Jim just lost it. He dropped the drinks, and the glasses smashed all over the floor. He launched himself at the guy who had spoken, laying in punches to his face, then he stood up, kicking him in the head. The guy's friend got up and tried to get Jim off but he was in too much of a rage to stop.

Katrina screamed, "JIM, GET OFF HIM!"

Two of the bouncers came running down and grabbed Jim and pulled him off. Jim was still screaming that he was going kill the man. The bouncers dragged him out through the side gate that led into the car park.

"Right, you, fucking calm down," one of the bouncers said. Katrina followed and grabbed Jim.

"What are you doing? have you lost your fucking mind!"

"Well, I take it he's with you? I suggest you take him home before he gets in some serious trouble," said the other bouncer.

Katrina took Jim by the hand, dragging him out, and sat him on the pub wall.

"What is wrong with you? He was just having a laugh and you have to go nuts. If this is the way it's going to be then I can't do this!"

Jim broke down. "I'm so sorry. He just got to me with his stupid mouth."

"I suggest you go home, and I've got to think about this. I'll call you tomorrow, and don't get in any more fights." Katrina then rang for a taxi. When it came, she got in and went without saying a word.

Jim banged his head with his fist. "Why? Why? Why?" he said in time with his fist striking his head. He took two bags of the speed, ripped them open and just stuck his face into them, sniffing the contents then licking the remnants, the sour taste making him wince. But he thought, "Fuck it; I've lost her."

Jim wandered the streets aimlessly, just thinking about the ultimate move – suicide.

"Would anyone miss me if I went? Probably a few, but not enough to make an actual dent in anyone's life."

The anxiety was exacerbated by the alcohol, the strong weed and the speed, which Jim was now coming up on. The streets were damp; there had been a light rainfall. Jim then wandered with pace through the park. His thoughts were as black as anything. And all the while, his mind was racing. He couldn't focus on just one thing as Katrina, suicide and song ideas were flooding his brain. Jim made his way home with these song ideas in his head, as he wanted to get them down. He stayed up that night, writing and playing and pacing round the house until the effects of the speed wore off and the come-down was getting worse. He was shaking, his mind still racing. He took one of his anti-depressants and had to just ride it out until he could finally get to sleep. As he drifted off, he suddenly felt a weight press down on the end of his bed. He could feel a hand on his foot. He lay there, petrified. The room's temperature fell to beyond freezing and Jim could see his breath being illuminated by the moonlight.

He then heard a familiar voice. "Hey, man, wake up."

Jim peered over the edge of his duvet and saw a dark shadow sitting at the end of his bed. Jim's petrified eyes tried to focus through the dark and saw that familiar face. Ben leaned forward. His features were a dark shade of blue and the cold-air steam from his breath was like it was mid-winter.

"You need to get a grip, man, for you never know when your last day will be."

The alarm went off. Jim awoke after only a couple of hours' sleep. He was shaking badly from paranoia, thinking about the vision. He said, "What the fuck is going on?" He was severely confused. And the thoughts of the previous night came flooding back. The fight with Katrina and her storming off also rattled his mind. Jim buried his face in his pillow and started to cry. He really wanted to get right, for he knew the drugs were feeding his anxiety, but he couldn't do without them.

Chapter 14

That day at work, Jim was a shadow of himself, looking pale and feeling sick. When Terry saw him, he said, "Fucking hell, what's were yous up to lasts night? You looks like complete shit."

Jim just sat there, staring into his coffee cup, shaking his head. "Oh, don't ask."

Terry just laughed. "A fews too many, I'ms is guessing. We've all beens there, but just don't makes it a regular occurrence."

Jim was in no mood to be told anything, especially in the manner of Terry's annoying speech impediment. Finally he made it through to the end of the day and he just wanted to go home and flake out, but on the way back he consumed some more speed, which wasn't ideal, but he had been just craving it all day. They all got together at the studio for a jam session later that evening. Jim's focus was not on the music and the others picked up on it.

"Jim, are you okay?" Tom asked.

"Yeah, just a few things on my mind."

It was Katrina on his mind, since she hadn't called that day like she said she would. And Jim didn't want to call her just in case he pushed her too far, but in reality, he wasn't prepared to hear what she had to say. He was very scared and paranoid. They just cracked on with the rehearsal, which was quite shaky, with Jim's inability to remember words and forgetting where to come in on parts. Jim introduced the others to the new songs he had written the previous night; they thought they were very dark. But they still liked them.

"Sure you're gonna be all right for Saturday?" Will said while rolling up a spliff of the crazy skunk weed.

"Here – have a grab on this. It will sort you out," Will said. That evening Jim finally got the phone call from Katrina. She told him that she needed a little more time just to think about things and that she still loved him and wanted to be with him, but he really needed to get help with everything. Jim agreed and said he would try. He apologised again for his behaviour and said he wanted her back so bad. He would do anything. The Saturday morning (the day of the gig), Jim was working on the till serving some customers when a guy came in. He was dressed in a well-pressed suit, his hair was slicked back and there was a rain coat sloping over his arm.

"All right, son, is Tel about?" he said in a thick cockney accent. Jim at once knew who this guy was. He looked your stereotypical London shady businessman, Jim thought. He resembled a character from *Only Fools and Horses* and Jim laughed to himself. Jim politely answered, "Hello, yes, he's just in the back. I will go and get him for you."

Jim wanted to make a good first impression.

Terry then arrived. "Hellos, Charlie, how's are you?"

"Not bad at all, me old mate. So where's this gig tonight?"

Terry told Charlie all about it and said that they'd go down together. He then introduced him to Jim.

"So, Charlie, this is Jim. He's the lad froms the band we're goings to see later."

"Agh, right. Well, hello again, I should say. I'm looking forward to coming down and watching you, see if we can get you something set up down in London."

Jim was completely taken aback with his comment, thinking "Wow, we're gonna play in London. Shit!"

They shook hands. Terry then decided to close up early, as it was unusually quiet for a Saturday afternoon. They headed down to the local café for a spot of lunch.

The café was quite full but they found a booth at the back. The aroma of bacon, sausages and fried eggs filled the room. Jim was ready with his order before they had even sat down. A full English was on the cards, with plenty of brown sauce and tea. Charlie took the lead with all the chat, asking Jim how long the band had been together, what gigs they had played and where he saw himself in all of it. Jim answered that that was all he and his friends had wanted to do; they were not interested in anything else, and that's how he saw his future.

Charlie said that he had heard from Terry about the death of his friend and was deeply sorry, explaining that all this knife violence was getting way out of hand and that stiffer sentences should be handed down. Jim agreed wholeheartedly.

Terry looked quite embarrassed by the fact that Jim knew that he had told Charlie about Ben's death. When Charlie excused himself to go the toilet, Terry apologised to Jim.

"I'm's so sorry for telling him. I justs wanted him to know your story and that's."

Jim put his hand on Terry's shoulder.

"Its fine, Terry, no need to apologise. I think he needed to know."

After lunch Jim made his excuses that he needed to go home and get ready for the gig and that he would see them down there later. The Phoenix was very hot that night; a lot more people were down than the previous gig. Will and Tom were setting up their instruments and getting ready, while Jim was writing out a set list on the spur of the moment.

Terry and Charlie walked over.

"Leaving that's a bits late, aren't yous?" Terry said about Jim writing the set list out at such a late hour.

"Agh, it will be fine; it's all the songs we know well anyway," Jim said.

Jim then called Will and Tom down and introduced them to Charlie. They all shook hands.

"Yeah I've come down to check you guys out, maybe get you down to London, like I explained to your boy Jim here." Charlie said.

Will and Tom both were now grinning from ear to ear at what they were being told. As they went back to their instruments, Tom said, "I just hope we don't fuck this up." They both glanced over at Jim, who had gone back to writing the set list.

Charlie then asked if any of them wanted a drink. They all said, "Yes!"

"Pints all round then, I'm guessing," Charlie said.

They raised their thumbs as a solid yes.

Across town Daz and Zack were parked up on country layby, getting ready for their first drug pick-up. A car came up behind them and its lights flicked off. A lone figure came to the window and knocked on it. "All right, lads, we've got your merch. You wanna flick your boot up?"

Zack got out and opened the boot. "Hello boys, how's things?" Zack said as he kept the guy talking who was loading the drugs into the boot. Daz got out and walked over to the guy loading the car. He pulled out a telescopic cosh and released it before cracking the guy over the head. He went down.

Another guy got out of the car and shouted, "What the fuck!"

But Zack was already on him, kicking the door into his chest and landing a crunching punch to the side of his head. He also dropped. Zack then picked him up and after banging his head against the roof of the car, he fell unconscious. Daz was laying the boot into the other one until he too fell silent. They then opened the boot of the other car to see what they had, and just as they thought, it was crammed with enough drugs to start their own empire, which was on their to-do list.

They took everything. They even found a money bag, which was packed with notes. They then loaded the two men into the boot of their own car and slammed the lid down. They both ran back to their car, got in and sped away, screeching the tyres into the night.

Back at the gig, Blue Veil Rain were rocking through their set, really getting the crowd going. When Jim looked out, he saw Keith in the background, and he waved. Jim nodded and smiled. Charlie was really getting into it and he let Terry know.

"Hey, Tel," Charlie shouted over the music, "these boys are pretty good." Terry looked at Charlie and smiled and nodded in appreciation.

After the show they got together for a drink. Jim invited Keith to come and have a drink and get something to eat.

"Hello, Keith, mate, how are you? Where's Patch?" Jim said.

"Oh, I tied him up outside. He should be all right. Anyway, great set, man. I really enjoyed your stuff."

Jim thanked Keith and then said to go and get his dog, that he couldn't leave him outside, as someone might nick him. Keith agreed and got Patch in. Tony got Keith and his dog some food and drink at Jim's request. Jim said to take it out of his share of the payment for the gig. But Tony said, "No, it's on the house."

Charlie gathered the lads round to discuss getting them down to London for a few gigs and said that he could sort them out as soon as possible. He said he would be in touch before ordering some more drinks for everyone. Keith was very appreciative and thanked them for their kindness. They were all having a good time with the post-gig drinks and smokes. Tom went out to the toilet and bumped into Katrina, who had just arrived.

"All right, Katrina. Jim's through there. He's been a right whining little bitch ever since you gave him the boot."

"I didn't; I said I needed time to think," Katrina said, quite annoyed with Tom's comment.

"Yeah, anyway, I need a piss," Tom said while bumping into the wall as he walked off.

Katrina blew out her cheeks. "Nice."

She went through. Everyone was getting a little rowdy, what with everything being consumed. Jim turned and saw Katrina walking in. He slid off his stool and went over to meet her.

"Hello, didn't think I was gonna see you for a while, if ever."

"Well, I see you haven't let that stop you doing what you want to do."

Jim looked at her with a frown.

"We've just played a gig, and we've been getting together after, like we always do. Look, Katrina, I'm so sorry for what I did. I was just a little messed up. And I don't want to lose you, but if all you've done is come down here looking for an argument, then I think you'd best leave. Or I will."

Katrina looked at Jim and smiled. "I'm not looking for a fight. I've thought about that night; you were just trying to protect me, in your own way." She laughed.

Katrina grabbed Jim, pulled him forward and kissed him. Jim wrapped his arms around her. "Whhhooooooooo" came from everyone at the bar and bursts of laughter.

Charlie said, "Get a fucking room."

Jim shouted, "Bollocks!" with a glazed smile etched on his face. He then took Katrina over to see Keith and Patch, who were propped up at the end of the bar.

"Hello there again," she said while giving Keith a big hug and bending down to fuss Patch. "How's it going? I hope all is okay."

Keith replied, "Yeah, as well as can be expected. We've had something to eat and drink, courtesy of your man."

Katrina turned to Jim and planted a big kiss on the side of his face.

"He's a good bloke, your Jim; keep hold of him," Keith said, nodding towards Jim.

As the night went on, and after much more consumption, Keith said his farewells along with Patch and they headed out into the cold night. Everyone else carried on having a few more drinks. Katrina was chatting to Terry and Charlie and having a laugh. One by one they started to disperse. Terry and Charlie then said their goodbyes.

Charlie grabbed Jim. "Great night tonight; superb gig. We'll catch up soon." He gave Jim a firm handshake. Terry too said his goodbyes and said that he would see Jim on Monday morning. Katrina took Jim back home, to make up.

Chapter 15

Daz and Zack were back at Daz's garage, which was part of his lock-up. They were sorting through the bags of drugs, checking each package. There were bags of Es, coke, speed, etcetera. To them, they had hit the jackpot. They broke open one of the bags of coke and did a few lines for celebration and quality control purposes.

"All good, I think," Daz said with a cheeky grin, his eyes glazed from the intake of the coke.

"We're gonna make a fucking fortune, and while we're at it, we'll run that old twat out."

Zack was so fucked from the drugs that he agreed with everything Daz said, even though he was reluctant before. They didn't take into account the heat they were going to get and what they had to prepare for. They were going to be hunted down.

The next morning, Jim awoke, feeling the effects of the previous night. He went down to make tea. The day was extremely gloomy. He kept thinking about those encounters with Ben; he was questioning the state of his mind.

"Was I awake, and it did happen, or was I semi-conscious? And was it a dream state, or am I just totally fucked up mentally?"

He felt he was turning into a paranoid mess with crazy illusions. He felt a hand on his back and spun round. It was Katrina.

"You okay? You seem very jumpy."

Jim's heart was racing; his anxiety was at a peak. He wiped beads of sweat from his forehead. "Yeah, I'm fine," he said, breathing heavily, "just in a bit of a daydream, looking out at this fantastic weather."

Katrina chuckled. "Yeah, not great, is it?"

As they made their way back up to bed, Katrina said, "Jim, I've got a serious question for you."

Jim's eyebrows rose. "Okay, and what might that be?" Jim was puzzled.

"Well, we've been together a bit now, and you spend quite a lot of time here. You have a job; you're too old to be living at home. So I just thought, would you want to move in here with me?"

Jim sat back. All these thoughts ran through his head.

"I get everything done for me at home – cooking, washing, etcetera, plus all my money's mine. That means I'd have to start paying out."

This didn't sit well with Jim, as he knew all his creature comforts would be gone, plus it was the weekend of Ben's funeral.

Katrina sat there staring at him. "You're very quiet; are you not into the idea?" She drank some of her tea. Jim just fidgeted with his cup.

"Well, it's a big step, you know, moving in together. I would really want to, but I don't know. You kind of threw me out with that question."

"Okay, just forget I said anything." Her annoyance was very clear. "I need to get a shower."

Jim sat back, blew out his cheeks and lit a cigarette. He felt real anguish over this, and he knew this could really progress their relationship. But he felt like he was drowning with the extra pressure he thought he would get with all of it. He felt Katrina's unhappiness. It was the last thing he wanted, especially with everything that had happened. And the thought that he had lost her once played on his mind, since it was his fault entirely that it had happened. He felt completely in her debt for taking him back, and that scared him. He just wanted to make her happy, but he didn't know if he had the strength to do it. He felt like a selfish prick, in that he wasn't considering her feelings.

When she came back from her shower, Katrina asked, "So have you thought any more about it?" Jim sat there, his mind still racing from the first time she had asked.

"Katrina, like I said, this is a massive step for me. I've never done this before. I really want to." He paused.

Katrina then spoke. "But you don't really want to. I'm taking you away from your freedom; I get it." She was clearly not happy with Jim's attitude.

Jim sat up. "No, I want to, I really do." He paused again, not really filling Katrina with any confidence about his commitment.

"Jim, I'm not getting any younger, and I thought we could have something. But if you're not man enough to do it then we should just call it a day, now!"

Jim was stunned.

"Well, I'm sorry for being such an inconsiderate fucking prick, but my mind is thinking about this weekend when we bury one of my best friends!"

Jim fell back against the headboard and dragged deep on his cigarette. He then pulled out his stash of weed and proceeded to roll up a joint, packing it fully. At this moment in time, he didn't really give a fuck, thinking, "Why the fuck should I bother when no one else does?" He was falling into a case of complete self-doubt he needed the strength for his friends funeral.

Jim was filled with a case of "No one understands" self-pity while smoking his spliff. Katrina walked back in the room.

"For fuck's sake, Jim, you said you'd never do drugs again. How can I trust you?" She turned out of the room, slamming the door.

Jim just sat there, smoking and thinking, "It is what it is."

Katrina came back into the room and apologised.

"I'm so sorry, Jim. I did completely forget about the funeral."

She sat down next to Jim, looking at him. She felt so ashamed of what she had said, "Jim, I'm so sorry for what I said; I was completely out of line."

Jim turned to her. He was now completely boss-eyed from the large intake of weed.

"It's okay," Jim said while falling back, completely stoned from that killer weed.

In that following week, it was all work, jamming, rugs (but only weed was accepted) and sex. (Weed was not an issue with Katrina now, just the chemicals.)

But Jim was sneakily taking speed behind Katrina's back and Will and Tom's backs, for they knew he was fucking up badly on it.

The morning of the funeral came. Jim woke with precision, as if he didn't need an alarm clock. He was completely on edge.

All that morning Jim paced up and down the landing. Katrina spoke to try and lighten the mood. "Be careful – you might wear the carpet out."

Jim was having none of it. He screamed at Katrina, "Why don't you just fuck off, if all you're gonna do is take the piss? One of my best friends is lying dead in a coffin because of some fucking prick who needs to be dealt with!"

He fell to the floor in a heap, crying. Katrina grabbed Jim, for she knew he didn't mean anything he had just said. He was just lashing out, and those circumstances justified his anger. She knew it and stood by him. Jim then stood up and looked out of the window at the weather. It completely identified with the state of his mood. The heavy rain was coursing down the window, cars were splashing puddles from the road up onto the path as people passed and collars and hoods were turned up to keep out the elements. Katrina and Jim made their way over to Jim's folks' house to get ready for the funeral, for his clothes were there. Jim's mum gave him a big hug as he came in. Tears were streaming from her eyes. Jim refrained from hugging his mum. He'd never done it before, so why start now? As they were sitting, waiting to leave, a knock broke the silence. Jim's mum went to go and see who it was.

"Jim," her voice bellowed into the kitchen, "Will and Tom are here."

Jim stood up and made his way to the front door. The temperature suddenly dropped.

Jim shouted to his mum, "Will you turn the heating up, please? I'm freezing." He then said, "All right, lads, come on in." They made their way to the kitchen, where Katrina was waiting. She greeted Tom and Will with a hug as they sat down. She was making tea for everyone.

Jim felt uneasiness within and couldn't get warm. "Is anybody else cold?"

They all said no, they were fine. Jim puzzled at this. All the windows were shut. He put his coat on and headed into the living room, where the fire was on. He was still so cold.

He just sat there looking into the flames, mesmerised by their hypnotic quality. Then he felt a draft eek its way under the living room door. It sent the temperature down so low he could now see his breath. Jim got up to go see where this was coming from, as all the doors, front and back, plus all the windows were closed.

He made his way to the kitchen again. "Anybody else here freezing cold?" he said, turning into the kitchen… but no one was there.

Jim then started shouting, "Hello? Where is everyone!"

He glanced out the back window to see if they had gone into the back garden, but no one was there. He then looked out the front and again – no one was there. He shouted up the stairs and went up to have a look round; still no one.

"Where the fuck is everyone?" He couldn't understand it.

Jim then heard a guitar playing from his bedroom, and he went over. Walking in, he said, "Oh, here you are."

But there was nothing, no one playing his guitar and nobody in his room. Jim scratched his head. "What is going on?"

The temperature of the room zeroed down to beyond freezing. Suddenly he heard the bang of his bedroom door being slammed. Jim just froze where he stood; he was too scared to look round. He then felt an icy-cold hand grab his shoulder. "Hey, man, why won't you look at me?"

Jim was now panicked, for he knew who was there. He closed his eyes tightly, wishing it away, thinking, "It's only a dream. It has to be."

Slowly he felt icy breath on the back of his neck as the figure moved round to face him. "Ben, why are you doing this to me?" Jim said, his voice in complete distress.

"I'm so sorry, Jim, but you were one of my best friends and I just wanted to see you before they bury me."

The tears were streaming down Jim's face. He opened his eyes to see Ben standing there, a big smile on his blue frozen face. He reached out to Jim and they hugged.

"Again, I'm sorry for putting you through this. I just needed this last time to say goodbye."

As they pulled back, the cold then seemed to dissipate a warmth blew on to Jims face, with Ben smiling, he nodded towards Jim" for this was a sign Jim believed for him to let him go, as Ben faded out, the homeless guy Keith stepped into view behind him, smiling and waving, carrying his dog, Patch. Keith called after him, "Jim, Jim."

Jim then awoke in the armchair by the fire. Katrina was shaking him. "Jim, Jim, wake up, it's time to go."

Jim just sat there, completely taken aback by the dream. He was frozen in his chair, thinking, "It was just a dream." Sweat was beading down his face.

Jim got himself together, more or less, and they made their way over to Ben's parents' house. The hearse was waiting outside. Jim, Will and Tom went over, each of them pressing their heads on the rear window, where the coffin was in view. Tears streamed down each of their faces, and they moved back to let Ben's parents be near their son. The procession moved out into All Saints' church for the service. The rain was still coming down. Jim, Will and Tom, along with Ben's brother and two of Ben's cousins, were the pall bearers. They made their way into the church, and the service proceeded. Jim scanned the room to see who was in attendance. The church was full with all of Ben's family and friends.

Jim then spotted Rob about halfway back, sitting with his girlfriend and a couple of friends. Jim was seething and nudged Will.

"You fucking see that?" Jim whispered.

"See what?" Will said.

"That cunt, Rob. How's he got the fucking nerve to come, when he just left Ben to die?"

"No matter what you think, Jim, they were friends as well as us. I don't like the prick either, but it's just the way it is."

It was a good send-off for their friend, even though the weather could've made the occasion better. They each placed a flower on the coffin just before it was lowered into the ground. Ben's mum let out a scream, falling into the mud, trying to claw her way to Ben's coffin.

"Let me go with him; I want to go!"

Ben's dad and a few others held her back and led her away. It was getting way too much for Bens parents Jim just glared at Rob. The wake was held at their local. Everyone went down for a few drinks and something to eat, even though not many of those who attended were really that hungry. Jim was drinking heavily. Katrina told him to slow down but he wasn't listening. Jim, Will and Tom did shots at the bar, saying Ben's name as each one went down.

Jim grabbed his pint and went to go sit by himself. Katrina grabbed his arm.

"Are you okay?"

Her sympathetic voice touched Jim. But he told her he just needed some time alone, just so he could process the whole situation and also try and figure out those visions that kept occurring. Was it really Ben trying to contact him, or just a wild, vivid dream? Also, that vision of Keith – what the hell was that all about? This whole thing was really freaking him out. Why was it happening to him? Jim reflected on all his issues and his drug use. He could only think that it had to be his drug use that was creating all these visions along with his already fragile mind. Or could it be just a last goodbye? He couldn't make any sense of what was happening.

Will then came over. "Hey, Jim, going for a smoke – you coming?"

Jim agreed. He wasn't feeling the best at present; the alcohol was taking effect. Tom broke out the cigarettes while Jim started skinning up a spliff; he needed something a little stronger. As they were chatting and smoking, Ben's parents came. They immediately put the spliff out. Ben's dad came over.

"You didn't need to put that out. I know you all do it. If it makes you feel good in any way, through all this, then do it. We thank you so much for coming."

Jim said, "We wouldn't have missed this for anything. Ben was one of us, and we were all friends."

He shook their hands and then made his way inside. It was then that Rob and his mates came rolling up.

"Jim, don't do anything, not today," Will said.

Jim nodded and turned away and they carried on talking, but Jim looked up because he heard the sound of laughing. Rob was joking around with his mates.

Jim just lost it. He broke away, ran up to Rob and cracked him in the jaw. Rob went sprawling onto the floor.

Jim screamed, "You, you fucking wanker, you ran off and left him there to die!"

Rob laying there, holding his face.

"Look, there was nothing I could've done. For fuck's sake, I didn't know where he was –"

Before he could finish, Jim laid the boot into Rob's stomach. Rob groaned with pain, as he was winded from the kick. Jim was still screaming, trying to get at him again, but Tom, Will and Katrina were holding him back.

"Jim, leave it!" Katrina shouted.

By this time, most of the pub had come running out to see what was going on.

Ben's mum ran over. "Please, stop it, please!" She grabbed Jim's arm.

Ben's dad ran over. "Come on now, lads, not now, not today. Just calm down!"

Rob had managed to get back up, still holding his face and stomach.

Ben's mum grabbed both Jim and Rob and pulled them together.

"Look, it's not any of your fault. You both were Ben's friends; he wouldn't want this. Please, shake hands; I cannot deal with this. Not today."

Fresh tears streamed down her face. Rob was still holding his stomach. His face was now swelling up. He held out his hand.

"Come on, man. Call a truce, for Ben's family and mostly for Ben."

Jim just stared daggers at Rob. He then turned to Ben's parents.

"I'm sorry for all that's happened now, but I cannot forgive this guy, and so I cannot shake his hand. It's just the way I feel and it won't change."

A single tear flowed down Jim's face.

"Anyway, I'll go now, let other people get to the bar." He smiled.

Ben's mum grabbed him and gave him a big hug and then turned to Rob and hugged him as well, along with Will, Tom and Katrina. Jim then started to walk away. Katrina shouted after him and ran to catch him up.

"Hey, wait up, I'll come with you," she said, just as Will and Tom came running up.

Jim then turned around. "Look, after everything that has happened today, I just need a little time to myself. I'm sorry; you guys go and do something."

He walked off, shoulders slumped over. He could not bear to be around anyone at this time; his mental state was going off the rails. Jim popped one of the happy pills into his mouth, just wishing for an effect to happen immediately. Back at the pub, the rest of the funeral guests were still standing around. Tom felt really shit about what had just happened, as they all did. But he spoke up about it.

"For fuck's sake, I just want this to be Over. I cannot believe what just happened. Today of all days."

Will then asked Katrina if she was okay. She said she was, but her answer sounded very doubtful.

Both Will and Tom tried to reassure her that everything was going to be okay and that Jim just needed some time by himself. But deep inside, Katrina was becoming unconvinced about Jim. He had said he would change, but through all this (although it was a very difficult time) she felt insecure about their relationship. They made their way back inside. Jim was making his way back home. He just needed some alone time after everything. He got back home and raided his dad's beer stocks from the fridge in the garage then made his way to his room. He sat there, and a numb feeling enveloped his entire being. He cracked open one of the cans and downed it in one then put on some music that would suit his mood.

He got a record out of its sleeve and then put it on the stereo.(The record was Stone Temple Pilots; the album was *Core*.) Jim loved the intro to 'Dead and Bloated'. He rolled up a spliff and was away.

All his thoughts just turned to Ben.

Chapter 16

That next morning, Jim's phone went off; it was Terry. He let it ring off. He couldn't stand to talk to anyone, as harsh as it sounded. Especially Terry – that voice went through him at the best of times, let alone now. A text then came through; it was again from Terry, explaining about how Charlie wanted them to go down to London to play some gigs.

This immediately got Jim's attention, but he was still in no mood for any conversation. Jim then texted Will and Tom about the message he had just received, but he still wanted some alone time to figure things out, mentally, not musically. They fully understood. Will then sent a message that Katrina was very worried about him and that he should contact her at some point to work things out and that he would be stupid to let that go. Jim pondered that thought but fell back to sleep. When he awoke again with the thought of Katrina, he felt so bad. He knew he was letting her down again and needed to fix it. He called her to let her know and that he was really sorry and that the situation had just got out of hand. He then told her about the London gigs being offered. She let him know her feelings and that she was finding it hard to be with him due to his volatile and unpredictable moods and told him to go to London to get out of the way for a bit, so they could both have the space to figure out what they really wanted.

That evening, across town, Daz and Zack were distributing their drugs (dealing). They didn't want any outsiders involved with what they were doing except for a few close, trusted people they would trust their lives with and they knew wouldn't rip them off. For Daz did explain (in his own unique way) what would happen if they tried anything stupid, such as going against them in any way, by producing a gun at the meet. Daz and Zack wanted it all for themselves. In Darren's eyes, the business was all too good, and he was not going to give it up at any cost. While they were sitting in the car waiting for their next customer, a lad came riding up on his bike. He handed them a note. "Who's this from?" Daz asked the kid.

"A couple of blokes down the road gave it to me; they said to pass it on to the two guys in the red Focus," he said before riding off.

They then knew they were being watched. Daz opened the note.

"You've got two days to hand it all back, the gear and all the money you took and all that you have made on top – call it interest." A bullet was stuck to the inside the note.

Zack got worried about this but put on a brave face to keep up appearances, even though he knew there would be reprisals for what they had done. Also, he knew that there would be a lot of attention from both the police and those they had stolen from. Daz seemed to get a kick out it, as if he wanted the danger and the notoriety.

He said to Zack, "Right, those fuckers want to play games? I'll give them a game to play."

Daz got out of the car and walked up to the rest of their crew, who were on the corners as look-outs, and told them to go to the pub around the corner and go to the car park and around the back to keep out of the way of the cameras. Once there, he told each one they were going to be tooled up, as a lot of trouble was going to come down. Out of the boot of his car he gave them all a weapon each, from baseball bats to knuckle dusters.

"Keep these safe and be a bit more vigilant than you usually would. We're being watched by them, so we've gotta watch each other's backs if we wanna keep this money rolling in. You understand me – they ain't getting fucking nothing back."

They were all in agreement. Zack was not feeling very confident at all. He didn't like this gangster attitude that his friend had;, he knew it wouldn't end well. But the money was too good to pass any of this up. But they were totally outnumbered; the odds were not in their favour. But Daz was now revelling in it. The drugs were making him go fucking insane; he thought he was some kind of Scarface figure. Well, he did revel in gangster films. He would constantly quote dialogue from certain scenes in those films. Zack was concerned that Daz was so far gone that he was confusing art with reality.

Chapter 17

The next day at work, Jim was doing the usual stuff. Terry had asked him to open up, as he had couple of things to do before he came in. When Charlie came in, his aftershave made Jim's eyes water, he had so much on. And it wasn't some Davidoff Cool Water or Calvin Klein. No, this was real old-school shit like Old Spice or Brut.

"Hello, lad, so did Terry let you know about the gigs I've got lined up for you?"

Jim smiled as he greeted Charlie.

"Hello, Charlie. Yeah, and I've let the others know and we're well excited for it. Thanks a lot for putting it together; it really is appreciated."

Charlie asked if Terry was around, and Jim said he would be in later, that he just had a few things to do before he came in.

"Okay, well I'll give Terry the details of dates and that. Oh, and also, I've set up a recording session with a guy I know, because I take it you haven't got anything down yet?"

Jim's eyes lit up even brighter. He said they hadn't and again thanked Charlie for everything. Jim was beaming; it was like all his Christmases had all come at once. As soon as Charlie left, Jim was straight on his phone to tell the others the update on their trip. There were immediate responses of massive excitement. He also texted Katrina to let her know, but there was no response. His paranoia was moving into overdrive he couldn't stand her not responding. He felt like he needed her approval. He then tried to call her but it went straight to answerphone.

Jim really didn't know how to get to grips with this. He still really loved Katrina and couldn't bear thinking she was with someone else. It all got the better of him, so after work he went down to the pub and drowned his sorrows and scored. When inside the pub, Jim targeted the pool table, but Daz and Zack weren't there. He thought that very strange. He ordered his drink and asked the barman if he had seen them around.

"No, they've not been in all day." He also noted this was very odd.

Jim made his way into the garden since he still had a couple spliffs' worth of weed in his pocket. His mind was racing with thoughts of Katrina being with someone else. He tried calling again but still no answer. He pondered on how his love life was so fucked up. The smoke was now getting to him, along with the booze. In the end he just thought, "Fuck it, she's gone." Just as he thought all his hope was lost, Terry rang and said that he had the dates for the gigs and that he would forward them to Jim. When they came through, Jim was gobsmacked. He thought there would be just a couple of dates. But no; they had two months down there, which included recording time. They would be going down there in two weeks, so they needed get their shit together. Jim started laughing, what with this news and being drunk and stoned. He let out a "Woo!"

The other people in the garden looked over with raised eyebrows.

Jim sat there laughing, staring at the phone screen and rubbing his eyes and staring again, as if to make sure it wasn't a hallucination or that he was dreaming it. He now had all this to occupy his time and get everything ready for the trip. This was an ideal time to get things straight and to get Katrina out of his mind. That night, while he was in the realm between sleep and consciousness, that cold drifted in again. His room turned a light shade of blue. This time Jim was not afraid, for he knew the figure at the end of his bed. He sat up smiling as the coldness of his breath blew out like smoke.

"Hello, Ben. Time for another visit?" Ben leaned forward. This time his face was normal, as if he were still alive. He told Jim that everything was okay and now to let him go but to still think of him from time to time, that he would never have another visit from Ben. Jim awoke to sunlight piercing through his curtains. The warmth and sense of calm enveloped him; it felt like a weight had been lifted from his shoulders. He also felt a great sense of happiness, which he hadn't felt in a long time.

At the end of the day, Terry spoke to Jim about going to London and asked him how he really felt about it.

"Well, I'm really excited by it, especially with the recording sessions being booked in as well," he said. "But I also have a sense of trepidation; things can also go tits up in the blink of an eye, so we don't really want to get too far ahead of ourselves."

Terry nodded in agreement. He was very impressed with Jim's mature attitude, for he knew it wouldn't be a an easy ride. Terry said, "Wells, anyway, I've got a little present for you. I knows it's a couple of weeks away, buts I thought I would gives it to you now."

Jim then followed Terry over to the electric guitars. Terry nodded at the burgundy Gibson SG Jim had been eyeing on his first day.

"There's you go, Jim; take it."

Jim was gobsmacked. "Are you serious? You're just gonna give me that guitar?"

Terry smiled. "Yes, it's a gift. I knows yous haven't worked here all that's long, but I have really enjoyed you working here, ands if it all works out, then I know you'll have the guitar you wanted, and if it don'ts, then you can give it me back." Jim shot Terry a stunned look. Terry laughed. "Only jokings. It's yours, plus you will always haves a job here."

Jim had to sit down. This was beyond friendship, and this was the best day of his life.

"Agh, man, I really don't know what to say."

"Then don't says anything. I can see hows you feel by that big smile and thats you nearly fell over when I nodded towards that SG."

A single tear fell down Jim's face.

That evening, Jim arranged a gig as a celebration for going to London. It was down at the Magazine bar, which was located about two hundred yards down from the Phoenix. It was also an incredible music venue. It was arranged for that weekend, and also as a first, this was going to their first headline gig. And so the rehearsals went on all that week, every night in the studio. Jim had been working on some new material and they also started to work on a couple more covers. They had 'Come as You Are' by Nirvana and 'Like a Hurricane' by Neil Young.

A new improved set was coming together. Also, the band discussed what songs they wanted to do for the recording sessions. The songs needed to be tight, and there being no fuck ups was key.

Tom added, "We need to do your song for Ben – that's a must."

Will nodded in agreement. Jim also agreed. He had never told anyone about those dream-state visits from Ben. He was still very confused by them, as he didn't know whether they were dreams or some sort of altered reality.

But in the end, he would put it down to all the drugs he was taking and the loss of a friend. The whole thing was messing with his mind. For the gig they decided just to do the songs ready for recording. They needed to be sharp, with a couple of covers thrown in for good measure. Jim told the others about the present Terry had given him.

"Fucking hell, Jim. Do you think he'll give me a new bass and Tom a new drum kit?" Will said, laughing along with Tom.

"Well now, you've gotta have the contacts that I have, and you have not," Jim said. A sarcastic smile was etched on his face.

Aghh, fuck off then, selfish prick," Tom said.

"Anyway, where were we?" Jim said to take their minds somewhere else, as they weren't getting any freebies.

"Okay, let's take it from 'Paranoid' then go from there. I think we ought to start with that. It is a bit of a crowd pleaser."

Will said like they had played it a hundred times before and they had a massive following. Jim just looked at him. "Crowd pleaser. We've only done two gigs, and we've only played that one at one of those," Both Tom and Jim started laughing. "Well, they seemed to like it when we did it; that's what I was getting at."

Jim nodded. "I get where you're coming from. Okay, cool; we'll start with that."

Chapter 18

Over the other side of town, Daz and Zack had gathered all their gang. It was decided to ambush those who had sent that message and basically send one back. They knew the location of the pub where they hung out, and they also knew exactly who they were. They pulled up a few hundred yards from the pub to hold back, so as not to be seen, when they saw a couple of the other gang coming out for a smoke.

"Right, lads get ready," Daz said as he snorted a big line of coke to get himself psyched up.

The gang donned their balaclavas and got out of the cars. They started to run in the direction of the other gang, ducking by the sides of the cars lining the street. A surprise attack was on the cards.

Before they knew what was going on, Daz had brought down his cosh right round one of their heads. He fell in a heap on the floor, just after another one of Daz's gang took out the other; he lashed the back of his legs with a baseball bat. The beating was relentless.

Just then the door opened and three more came out. Zack grabbed one of them, smashing him round the face with his knuckle duster. The blood sprayed across the pub wall. The others laid into the other ones who had come out.

Daz then shouted, "Right, that's enough!"

He picked up the one he was beating, pulled out his Glock pistol from inside his coat held it to the guy's head.

Daz said, "Right, you go back and tell your fucking boss, I don't like being handed threats. Tell him to steer clear of me or there's gonna be a fucking war!" He threw the guy down before heading back to his car. Daz was beaming, grinning from ear to ear. "Wow, that felt good." Zack didn't say anything. He just smiled and nodded in agreement.

Chapter 19

The next morning Jim was awoken by his mobile ringing. It was Katrina.

"Hello, Jim, how are you? Sorry to call so early."

"Hi, I'm okay. I didn't think I was going to hear from you again."

There was a bit of a pause. "Errm, I have something to tell you. And I'm not sure how to say it but –"

Again a prolonged silence.

"Yes, what is it?" Jim said, concerned about the answer.

"Okay, I will just say it. I'm pregnant."

Jim fell back on to his pillow, totally freaked out at what she just said, planting his hand to his forehead. He blew out his cheeks.

"Hello? You still there?" Katrina asked. She was now panicked by his silence. "Jim, say something."

Jim took a few deep breaths. "Hello. I'm sorry; I just was not expecting that. Well, I don't hear from you in a while and then you hit me with this."

"You want her back, you fucking idiot, and you say that?" he thought to himself.

"I'm sorry, Katrina, I didn't mean it the way it came out. It was just a complete shock. I really thought you were gonna say that you've thought about everything and you want to leave it because of my stupid attitude."

Katrina laughed, which was a good sign.

"No, you idiot. I did a test yesterday and it came back positive, so I had to let you know. Are you mad that I've told you?" Her voice was trembling.

"No, of course I'm not; you just threw me out. I'm fucking happy."

"Could we meet up and properly discuss what we should do?" Katrina said, her voice now calm.

Jim agreed. They met up in town at the McDonalds on the high street. Jim gave Katrina a big hug when he saw her. They sat for about ten minutes before either of them said a word. Katrina then asked Jim if he wanted to keep the baby and said that she would keep it anyway, even if he didn't want to have anything to do with it.

Jim shook his head. "Of course I want to keep it. Have you told your folks about it?" Jim asked.

"Yeah. My mum is really pleased. Even though you haven't met she knows all about you, so now you're gonna have to meet." She laughed.

"And your dad?" Jim said, a slight panic in his voice.

"Well, I've asked my mum to tell him because I'm a little unsure about his reaction."

Jim took a deep breath and drank down the last of his Coke.

"I see," he said, raising his eyebrows. Jim then told Katrina about the gig at the weekend, down the Magazine bar, and said it would be great if she could come down.

"It's our celebratory gig before London." Jim then paused, burying his head into his hands. "I can't go now; that's right out of the question."

Katrina grabbed his hands. "You are going and that is final. You've been wanting this for so long; you need to go."

The guilt about going welled up inside Jim. He was completely torn. That evening, Jim called his folks and told them about the news. His mum screamed down the phone with complete elation and not anger. His dad said, "Oh son, you've fucked your life now. Congratulations anyway." The tone said it all.

Will and Tom were really pleased for them, after Jim told them. They told him so in their unique but immature way.

"Jim, you dirty bastard, but congrats anyway," said Tom.

"Fuck's sake; you with a kid?" Will said with a lot of sarcasm.

All agreed to go for a drink to celebrate after work. Jim told Terry, who expressed his congratulations by giving him the next afternoon off. When at the pub, Tom pulled Jim to one side.

"So is London out of the question now? I don't want to sound out of line or anything, but you know, it did cross my mind."

Jim paused. "Well, I thought the same, but Katrina insisted we all still go down, because it's something that we all want."

Tom nodded. "Wow, she's very understanding. Most girls would be holding you back, saying, that's it, the thumb permanently crushing the top of your head."

Jim laughed. "Yeah, I know."

Jim's parents came into the pub and hugged Katrina, saying congratulations and everything. Jim's mum asked if Katrina's folks were coming down.

"No, they're not. It's a bit too far for them to come up here, but my mum's okay with it, but my dad's quite stubborn, and when he heard, he was not best pleased," she said. looking to the floor.

Jim's dad said, "Well, to be honest it's quite understandable; Jim has never met your parents, has he? And you both shoot this out of the blue." Jim's dad shot from the hip when he spoke, one of those, "If you're not going to be honest then don't say anything."

Jim's mum gave him a daggers stare, shook her head and downed her gin and tonic, with one gulp.

Embarrassment was etched over her face.

Jim's dad just shrugged his shoulders. "Well, anyone for another?" he said and he downed his pint.

The mood became quite frosty towards Jim's dad, but everyone took advantage of his offer. Jim turned to Katrina. "So, I guess we'll be moving in together after all." He laughed.

Chapter 20

The night of the Magazine gig arrived. Tom, Will and Jim were getting all their stuff into the side entrance, where the stage was, when a man came up and asked one of the bar staff if Jim Staley was about. The man pointed towards the stage.

"He'll be over there, loading all the stuff onto the stage."

The man wandered over. "Hello, could you tell me which one is Jim?"

Jim looked up. "I'm Jim. Who are you?" Jim spoke with suspicion, thinking, "Shit, what have I done?"

"Hello, could I have a word in private?"

Jim made his way down towards him. "Right, lads, be back in a minute."

Standing by the bar, the man introduced himself as Fletch.

"I work for one of the homeless shelters in the town centre." He asked Jim if he knew anybody called Keith. Jim nodded.

"Yeah, we did meet a guy on the street called Keith. He had a dog called patch, came down to one of our gigs, nice man. We gave him and his dog something to eat."

Fletch said, "Yeah, Keith talked about you and your girlfriend, Katrina. He said that you were both nice people and that you were in a band called Blue Veil Rain; that's how I found you. I saw the ad for the gig and decided to come down to let you know."

Jim suddenly felt uneasy, as if he knew what was coming.

"You see, Keith never had any family that we knew about; he never talked about his past. So we didn't know who to contact family-wise. He only talked about you, your girlfriend and your band."

Jim had a swig of his beer, scratching his head.

"Okay, so what's happened to him that you needed to contact his family?"

Fletch paused. "Well, we were doing our rounds as we do each night, checking on each individual homeless person, checking on their welfare and that, and when we came to Keith, he was lying in his sleeping bag, We tried to wake him, but there was no movement. We checked his breathing." Fletch bowed his head and with a deep sigh said, "There was no pulse, nothing. So we called an ambulance, but unfortunately we were too late. He was declared dead on arrival. They say it was more than likely hypothermia."

Even though Jim had only known him for that brief time, he was still quite shocked.

"Oh no; he was a really nice man. What about his dog?"

Fletch again looked down.

"His dog also perished; it looks like they were trying to keep each other warm."

"So when did this happen?" Jim said, an air of sadness in his voice.

"We found him last Wednesday morning."

Jim thought about it and realised that was the night he had that last visit from Ben and then saw Keith as well.

"Did I have a premonition or something?" Jim said to himself, unable to grasp what was going on.

Jim slipped into a panic attack. He felt himself unable to breathe properly. Fletch asked him if he was okay. Jim then ran outside to get some air. He sat on the steps round the back of the venue, just to be alone and get his bearings.

He couldn't believe what he had heard. "It was just a crazy drug-addled dream. It isn't possible. It just cannot be real," he kept repeating to himself.

Katrina then came round and found him sitting there rocking, still repeating this line.

"Hey Jim, are you okay?" A worried look crossed her face.

Jim was just staring into space, as if no one was in there. The others, including Fletch, came out.

"What's wrong with him? Is he okay?" Tom asked, looking deeply concerned about his friend. He had a look of, "Well we've seen this before," while blowing his cheeks out with a deep breath. Will then turned to Fletch.

"What the fuck did you say to him?"

Fletch explained about Keith and that he was down to let Jim know and that as soon as he told him, "He just went very pale then ran out."

Jim then broke from his trance.

"I'm okay. Can everybody just leave me alone for a moment? I just need to get my shit together."

As the others all made their way back inside, Jim produced a little cellophane bag with a couple of grams of coke in it, which he still had from his last meet with Daz and Zack, whom he had bumped into a few days before. After all the promises he had made to Katrina, he couldn't get free of his love for the drugs. He felt deep shame; he felt like a complete liar for this deception, especially with a baby on the way. The pickup was almost instant. he made his way back inside, with his attitude completely turned around.

Now he was racing, ready to get it on and play. Will and Tom were both suspicious of such a quick bounce back. Katrina was over by the bar, where she could sit down. They kicked into 'Paranoid'. The crowd went nuts, as the performance now included Jim, with a stage presence, going crazy on stage, jumping around and screaming into the mic. But this was a purely drug-fuelled show, unbeknownst to everyone except Will and Tom, who knew all the signs. Terry then showed up with Roger, the dickhead who had caused the problem for Jim on his first day at the shop. Jim clocked them coming in and nodded towards Terry. Terry waved back; Roger raised a glass towards Jim. Jim sarcastically smiled back. He was reminded of his humiliation on that day, so he decided to reciprocate. Halfway through the third song he slung his guitar behind his back.

"Well, we have a lot of people in here tonight, a great crowd. I'd like to personally thank everyone for coming down."

He then went on about how this was a celebratory gig, for they were going to London for gigs and recording.

"But there is a special person here tonight, and, well –"

He paused a second.

"I work at the music centre in town, and on my first day, this self-righteous, over-confident twat came in. He started baiting me about how I knew nothing and that I would get his order all wrong. So I gave it back to him. He didn't fucking like that, did he? So he gave me that killer line: 'Do you know who I am?' So I told him, no; who are you?" The crowd started to boo, whistle and laugh. "He didn't like that. He went on that he was this big star but got told that he was a massive bighead because he had a minor song in the seventies and had been living off it for all this time. I just laughed at him. Ohh, that got him mad, and he stormed out."

Will and Tom were looking at each other, knowing the story and laughing along. Terry looked stunned, for knew what was coming. Roger's face was red and heated. "Well, you know what? The guy's here tonight."

Jim then asked the lighting guy to shine a spotlight over by the bar and told him when to stop. When the light passed over Roger's face, Jim shouted, "STOP! That's the guy, everybody, Mr fucking do-you-know-who-I-am."

Everyone turned around, laughing at him. People were shaking their heads and sly remarks were being made as Will and Tom kept the rhythm going through this tirade. Both were grinning from ear to ear.

"Well, Roger, here's a big fuck you for trying to embarrass me. Karma's a bitch – didn't you know?"

Roger glared at Terry as though he knew he had told Jim about him and all that stuff from back then. Jim looked back over at the bar. Roger seemed to be waving an accusing finger towards Terry. But Terry just stood there taking it, as though he knew this was coming.

As the band carried on playing, Jim felt bad for Terry and that he had put him in that situation, but at the same time was glad he did it. After his outburst, he couldn't let it drop.

The set went on without incident, apart from a few forgotten lyrics and missed notes – all the joys of live music. As it came towards the end, Jim broke out his old acoustic, announced that they were going to be doing a song about a dearly departed friend, and he and Will sat down on the drum riser. Jim strummed the first few notes, Will came in with a low bass tone, while Tom played a slow cross stick, which in turn brought out the vibe of the song. The audience were really getting into it. There were a few tears from some of the people they knew who also knew Ben. A light beamed past the band. It was something they didn't know was going to happen. As they all looked round, a big picture of Ben was streamed across the back wall. They froze for a split second as it sunk in. Jim gulped at the sight. Each of them had to try and hold it together. For Jim, the face up there cast his mind not just to remembering those times with his friend but also those visits in the night.

Jim bowed his head and played on with all the emotion he could muster, before then standing up. He took his acoustic to the back of the stage and told the others to keep playing.

He picked up his electric guitar, the burgundy Gibson SG, and began running through the chords. He stepped on the fuzz pedal, cranked up the volume from his guitar and moved up to the mic.

"Play fucking louder!" Jim instructed the others.

Will and Tom understood. Tom crashed his cymbals while Will started playing heavy on the bass, and they rocked that fucking song out. That's what Ben would've wanted. After running through the last of the song they rang it out, just going crazy, making as much noise as possible. Jim then shouted, "This fucker's for you, Ben; rest easy, my friend."

The crowd went nuts. This was the best yet.

That was the feeling Jim wanted all the time. He thought about his old friend, wondering where he could be, if anywhere. As the lights went up, a very disgruntled, drunk Roger approached the stage.

"What the fuck was that all about, embarrassing me like that, you little shit!"

Jim just stood there, dislodging the mic from the stand. He just glared at Roger while looping the mic cable. Jim put it down and jumped from the stage in front of Roger.

"Well, I explained everything up there. Didn't it sink in with you, or are you just too fucking stupid to fully understand?"

Roger was fit to burst; his anger levels were breaching the safe point, so to speak.

He then lunged towards Jim, grabbing him by the throat. Both fell to the floor with an exchange of punches. Terry ran over as a couple of doormen came through to break it up. Terry grabbed Roger but was bundled out the way by the oncoming doormen, who in turn picked them both up, dragging them out. Roger was still screaming that he basically wanted to kill Jim. On the other side Jim was laughing. He just found Roger to be absolutely insane and saw the funny side.

Jim shouted to Will and Tom, "Right, lads, I will see you in a bit."

Will looked over at Tom and just shrugged. "Well, looks like it's just me and you then to clear away."

Terry came over. "Right, lads, do yous guys need a hand, since you're a mans down?"

Tom laughed. "Yeah, thanks a lot."

"Getting quite regular now, Jim getting into bother," Will said. raising his eyebrows.

"I guess he just wants to gets out of all the clearings up," Terry said with complete sarcasm. Will and Tom both looked at each other laughed and, shrugging their shoulders, agreed with what Terry had said.

Chapter 21

The day came for the London trip. Jim was all prepared to the amazement of his mum, who was not really happy, what with Katrina being pregnant and that, but she was well aware that Katrina was totally fine with it all and that she had told Jim to go. The way down was an experience for both the lads and the commuters on the train, as Will had brought a bag of booze for the trip down. It was no small carrier bag: it was his big rucksack, which had all his clothes and a special compartment for the drink. It weighed quite a bit, but this was of no concern to Jim and Tom, as they didn't have to carry it. The carriages were pretty crowded. Jim's anxiety was starting to flare up, and he was pretty quiet. He felt eyes all over him. He made his way to the toilet to get out of the way of everyone. He took one of his tablets to try and stabilise himself, and he took a few deep breaths. He was thinking, "Not now, please."

The noise from the carriage grew ever louder outside the door. Jim was holding his head; he just needed some quiet. It was a suffocating experience, feeling the claustrophobia as the noise just grew. A bang on the door broke Jim out of his situation.

"Hello, who's in here? You've been in here long enough. There are other passengers, you know!"

Jim sat there shaking as the banging continued, gripping his hair, saying to himself, "Just shut the fuck up. Just go away; leave me alone!"

He watched the tracks through the open window, hypnotising him. He thought that if he could squeeze himself through the window and fall onto the tracks then it would all end. He couldn't help the tears now flowing down his face. The guy was still outside, shouting for him to get out. Jim then heard the voice of Will outside, having a heated conversation with the man, then telling the man to fuck off and leave it. The man shouted to Will that he was going to tell the inspector and get them thrown off. A sudden calm came over Jim in that second, like in the eye of a storm, as he found the exchange quite funny, laughing through his tears.

"Hello, Jim, mate, you in here?"

Jim then opened the door. His face was red and patchy from crying.

"Fucking hell mate, you okay?"

"Yeah, I'm okay. I just got a little overwhelmed when we got on, with so many people on board."

Jim could tell Will had had a few from the way he was talking and swaying (and it wasn't just the swaying of the carriages).

"Well, I heard your little exchange with that guy banging on the door."

Will just nodded. "Well, he was harassing you, so I just told him what to do, even though I didn't know you were in here. It could've been anybody." Will shrugged. "Anyway, he's just gone to get the inspector."

Jim laughed. "Yeah. I know. I heard. Anyway, got any more booze for me?"

The man Will was baiting came back down with the inspector, pointing out Will as the main culprit, who had, as he put it, threatened him. The inspector questioned Will about the incident, and Will confessed to it.

"Yeah, I did it, but this prick was harassing my friend here," Will said, putting a protective arm round Jim, keeping him close as if to shield him from anybody on that train. The man's face grew red; he grimaced with every word Will was saying. All the while, Tom was keeled over laughing.

"My friend was not feeling well, so he just needed to go, and like I said, this guy was properly harassing him."

The inspector turned to the man.

"Well, is this true? Were you harassing this lad like he said?"

"Well, I didn't know he was inside and didn't feel very well. I just thought he was messing around. I knew he was with them making all the noise and drinking."

Tom had transferred the cans into another bag and slid them under his feet and proceeded to kick them back further under his seat just in case the inspector tried to search for them. The inspector said that he could smell the alcohol on their breath and wanted to search the contents of their bags.

Jim then said, "We're not drinking now; we were at the station though."

The inspector searched all their items but didn't find their drink.

"Okay, well, any more and you're off. That goes for you too, SIR!" the inspector said, turning to the man. When he was gone, all three of them burst out laughing and the man went off huffing back to his seat. The other passengers got back to what they were doing. There were a few laughs from the younger people and some stern looks from some of the elderly who had nothing better to do than stare and make sly comments. Tom then whipped out the bag and passed round some more cans. Will complimented Tom on keeping them concealed so as not to get thrown off. That was the last thing they needed. The train pulled into Euston Station, where Charlie was waiting for them.

"All right, lads, how was the journey down? All good I hope?"

"Yeah, not too bad, except for this dickhead harassing Jim," Tom said.

"Why, what happened?" Charlie asked.

Will then proceeded to tell Charlie about all that went on coming down.

They all piled into Charlie's car to go where they would be staying. Charlie's car really suited his style: it was a 1968 Jaguar XJ6. They arrived at the flat just outside Pimlico. It was a half-decent place for them to stay but a far cry from some of the posh gaffs they had passed on the way. The three of them gazed and dreamed.

"One day," said Jim.

They had the flat for all the time they would be there. It was one of Charlie's properties; he would let it to the artists he represented. They were shown around the flat. It was a spacious three-bedroomed place with a half-decent view from the front and back bedrooms, and the other was a side room, which faced a brick wall. So they decided to toss a coin for who had what. Will ended up having the side room – he told the others they were complete wankers.

Jim had the front room, so he was well made up. He called Katrina and told her about the journey down and about the place they were staying, and he said that he hoped she would come down soon. She said she hoped to at the weekend. She told him that she had talked to her parents and that they were coming round to the idea that they were going to be grandparents.

Jim laughed. "That's good then. Just gotta get my old man on board, or just leave it to my mum; she's better at that."

That evening Charlie took them out on the town, showing them the sights and around a few of the places they would playing, meeting the gaffers of each venue. No doubt it was going to get really messy, as they more or less had free drinks at every pub, which Jim and will took complete advantage of. But Tom, on this night, was more laid back. he wanted to savour every moment. Charlie had some good contacts, so that made it all so much easier.

Chapter 22

A text came through on Daz's phone. It was a message from one of Derrick English's associates, saying they wanted a meet that night at eight thirty so that they could work something out, and that all this trouble was just getting everybody nowhere. They didn't want any more violence; they just wanted to get straight without any more hassle and see if they could come to a resolution and get back to business. The meeting was to be held at the same place as the original meeting.

"This is a fucking set up," Zack said to Daz.

"We can't go; it would be suicide."

Daz took another line of coke. "Well, we'll go and see, won't we," he said, wiping his nose and constantly sniffing. His mind was going completely off the rails.

"Right, get your shit together. We're going over there to see what they've gotta say."

Daz felt over-confident about dealing with this guy, so much so that he intended they go in alone, much to Zack's protests.

"Shouldn't we get everyone together? You know, just in case."

Daz gripped the sides of Zack's head.

"You worry too much, my son. Just me and you. That will send a clear message that we don't give a fuck. We will walk in there, and they'll shit it, because they'll be fully manned and will expect us to be as well."

Daz smiled, his eyes bulging from all the coke he was doing. He had a couple of pistols tucked away in the wardrobe of his bedroom, which he showed to Zack and told him to try them, get a feel for them, for when it came time. Zack complied and took to shooting a few bottles in Darren's garden, feeling very uncomfortable. Daz looked at his friend firing off a few shots and grinned. He put his arm round Zack's shoulders.

"We'll get down there early doors and hide the guns in the toilet."

"That's a bit *Godfather*, Daz" Zack said with a frown.

Daz grinned an evil grin. "The fucking *Godfather* has nothing on me, pal."

Zack nodded. "Whatever, mate. I'm sure you have it figured out."

When in the car, Daz said there were a couple of shotguns in the boot.

"We could pick up a couple of trench coats from the army surplus store to hide the shotguns under."

Zack looked dismayed and said, "Don't you think they'll search us first?"

Daz laughed. "I thought the same thing, so we'll just leave them in the boot."

Zack shook his head.

"Come on, let's just get this over and done with."

When they stepped inside the place, it was all pretty quiet. A few punters were sitting round the bar but no one they recognised. They ordered a couple of drinks. It was still about fifteen minutes before they were to have the meeting and so Daz made his way into the back, where they had had the meeting before. There were some toilets nearby, so he went in and stashed the guns in one of the cubicles behind the tank. He had just got back to where they were sitting when a man came over. He told them Derrick had just turned up and to follow him to the room. As they entered, they saw those familiar faces from the last time. All of his crew were there, plus some others they didn't recognise. Daz smirked at Derrick as they entered the room.

They all sat down at the table, which was one of those big boardroom-type business tables. Derrick ordered drinks to be brought in: expensive wine, brandy, vodka, etcetera, and trays of cocaine. All the curtains were drawn, the big red drapes blocking out all of the outside world so complete privacy could be observed.

"And so we meet again, but now under unfortunate circumstances," Derrick said while pouring some wine. "Please, help yourself," Derrick said, waving an offering hand to them.

Daz went for a large brandy while Zack poured himself a vodka Red Bull.

Derrick leaned back in his chair.

"You know what. Darren, my boy…"

Daz hated being called Darren, and also being called "my boy" was a major insult, and his face showed it.

"I'm not mad about you taking all my stuff from me," Derrick said, lighting a big cigar.

"I was at the start, you know, when it first happened, but not now," he said, bringing both hands up as if to say, whatever. Daz was surprised by this comment and paused with the tip of the glass to his lips. He then put the glass down.

"Oh really? Why are you not now?" He asked the question with deep suspicion.

"Because I find strength in you, a serious attitude that not many people possess; what you want, you will get, no matter what; a definite attribute you need in this business."

Daz sat there, a look of bravado etched on his face, like he was some kind of god.

"Well, I feel some kind of proposal coming on," Daz said, sipping his brandy.

Derrick smiled then whispered to one of his men, who quickly went off into another room and returned with a briefcase, which he placed in front of Daz.

"Well, what is this?" Daz said, his hands held aloft.

"Open it," Derrick said, cradling his glass of wine.

Daz was extremely suspicious. "It's not gonna blow up in my fucking face, is it?"

Derrick laughed. "Well, if it was a bomb, do you really think I'd still be this room?"

The whole room then filled with laughter. Daz then opened the briefcase, eyeing everyone in the room. He looked inside, and his eyes widened. It was filled with money.

Daz looked around, still with an air of suspicion.

"Well, what's this for?"

"I want us to be a partnership. I could really use someone like you. You have your own crew, who I understand are fully capable when doing certain jobs, so we could destroy all those little fuckers who came to the last meeting and take their business for ourselves."

Daz smiled. "Do you mind?" he said, picking up one of the trays of coke.

"Be my guest," Derrick said before taking a big gulp of wine, emptying the glass.

"Right, shall we shake on this deal?" Derrick said while pouring himself another glass of wine. Daz looked up, his pupils severely dilated, laughing manically, and offered some to Zack, who refused. He was just sticking with his vodka. They all stood up and shook hands and hugged. Derrick stared into Daz's eyes.

"This is a great fucking day; we're gonna make a lot of money."

Daz whooped. "It certainly is, my friend, and I cannot wait to get what's coming to us." Daz's arrogance was still at the forefront; he now felt untouchable.

Derrick smiled. "Oh, don't worry; something very exciting is coming to us and especially to you, Darren, my boy."

Derrick looked past Darren's shoulder and nodded, at which Darren turned round. Then two faint shots rang out. Daz stood there for a moment a stunned look etched across his face, with two holes in his head that started to seep, before falling face first onto the floor, blood oozing from his head.

"Now get this piece of shit out of my sight. Fucking rip *me* off," he said while giving Darren's body a kick. Four of his men rolled Daz's lifeless body in the rug he had collapsed on and took him away.

"Well, my boy, good job. Now that money's all yours, so just take it and go."

Zack picked up the case. He still had the gun in his hand. Smoke emanated from the silencer. "Well, what shall I do with this now?" he asked, holding the gun up.

"Well, I would advise you to take it as far away as possible and throw it into the deepest water you can find."

Zack took the hint and left. Once outside he threw up into a drain. He never thought he could do that, especially to his friend. But there was no way he could let things carry on the way they were going. He felt a huge sense of guilt about all the pain he and Daz had inflicted on people. Zack was more than happy being a low-key dealer, making quite a bit of money just through that. But this was too much.

Zack had made a deal with Derrick some time before to give back all that they had taken and also to get rid of his best friend. Now he just wanted clear of this place, to start anew elsewhere.

Chapter 23

The following morning back in London, Jim was just waking. The sun shone through a gap in the curtain, resting directly on his face. He waved his hand to shield his eyes from the blinding rays. His head was banging from the night before. He heard Will making his way to the toilet. There was a silence before Jim heard the heaving sound of Will throwing up all of the previous night's activities. Jim lay there laughing, gripping his head with every laugh, as it was banging. He finally made it down the stairs to find Tom making breakfast. He was completely fine.

"Are you having a fucking laugh?" Jim said, looking at the eggs frying in the pan. Tom just stared at Jim.

"Well, I didn't put away half of what you two idiots did, but it was funny to watch."

Jim made it through to the living room, which looked like a bomb site. Beer cans and wine bottles were strewn over the floor; cigarette butts and spliff roaches were overflowing in the ashtrays, a couple of pizza boxes were discarded on the living room table. He just shook his head and then fell onto the sofa. He wasn't at the races at all today. Tom emerged from the kitchen with his plate of fried-egg sandwiches.

Jim couldn't look. The TV had the morning news on with a story about another bombing in the Middle East and politicians lying about everything they intended to change for the better.

"Beautiful day outside; we should make the most of it," Tom said, all enthusiastic.

"No way, man. First thing I saw this morning was a sunbeam through the curtains. It seemed like the curtain wanted me to suffer, so it opened just enough to let that beam directly into my eyes."

Tom looked at him with a frown. "So you think there's a conspiracy between the curtain and the sun to make your life hell?"

Jim pondered that thought. "Well, yeah, I think there could be."

Tom threw a sock at Jim's head.

"You are a twat, mate. Anyway, we've got that gig tonight down in Camden," (even though Camden's north of Pimlico) "so you better get yourself capable for that."

Will then emerged, still looking decidedly green.

Tom looked up.

"Egg sandwich?" he said with a smirk.

Will raced to the kitchen and another volume of puke fountained over the sink and onto the window. He fell down next to fridge, opened up the freezer compartment and pulled out a bag of frozen peas, resting it against his head. As Tom made his way back into the kitchen, he saw Will lying next to fridge with the bag of peas stuck to the side of his face.

"Oh my fucking god; you as well?"

Then seeing the sick over the window he said, "Well, I am not cleaning that up," and made his way back upstairs for a shower. A few hours later, when Jim and Will were reasonably normal, they headed to the tube for a trip round the capital to check out the sights and head to the place they would be playing to get a clear-headed view of the inside. That evening Charlie came by to pick them up, loading all their stuff into his boot.

"Hey, I've got a little surprise for you guys when we get down to the pub."

All looked slightly puzzled by what it could be. Jim just smiled and raised his thumb. "Cool." The set-up for the night was amazing. The lighting for the gig was "fucking great!", as Will eloquently put it. There were three others on the line up, Blue Veil Rain were to be first up on the bill. The sound check ran pretty smooth; no major problems. They kicked off with 'Paranoid' and ran through the set. Jim was excelling at his stage presence. He wanted to make the biggest impact, for they knew this could launch them. And that first night it did. It automatically created a buzz. People wanted to talk to them after their set, about where they came from, how long they'd been going, etcetera. They were "made up to fuck!", as Jim stated to Charlie, issuing another set of thank yous for getting them down to play.

Charlie then said about the surprise for them.

"Right, lads, come with me." They followed him through to the back of the pub to a quieter area. Charlie led them to a table where a man, around mid-thirties, sat nursing a glass of whiskey. Charlie then introduced them.

"Okay, lads, this is Quinney, Gary Quinn, hence the nickname Quinney. He's gonna be your producer, engineer and all that, for what's gonna be your debut master piece."

"Hello, lads."

Quinney reached out to shake their hands. "I'm looking forward to working with you. Any friend of Charlie's is a friend of mine."

They all sat down, each introducing themselves. Quinney said how much he liked their set; he said he loved the intro song.

"Always been a massive Sabbath fan; very nice touch."

He was also impressed by the song they did for their late friend.

"We can really work on that, make it stand out. Great song guys, I mean it."

Charlie went on to explain all about his years working in music, studying sound engineering for a time and gaining his skills through on-the-job training with engineers in and around London. He spoke about the studio and all the equipment they'd be using, which completely went over their heads, for they didn't have a clue about the different mics and how everything was set up to create different sounds, the mixing desk and so on. They sat like three nodding dogs watching a bone moving up and down in front of them, a glazed look across their eyes. "The recording sessions will start on Monday at ten on the dot, so make sure you're capable. Anyway, I'll be down for your next gig tomorrow."

Chapter 24

A dog sniffing through the undergrowth on his daily walk came to an abrupt stop. He picked up a scent from up in the trees, barking towards the object up there. His owner came up to see what all the fuss was about. He glanced up in the direction where his dog was looking, thinking he had picked up a squirrel or something.

"Jesus!" he screamed while falling back, his face now white as a sheet.

Up there amongst the branches was a hanging body. It was rocking back and forth, hitting the tree trunk in the stiff breeze, the face obscured by the thicket of leaves. The man fumbled for his phone, which tumbled from his pocket onto the dewy grass. He picked it up and with shaky hands typed in 999.

"Police, please. Hello? I want to report a dead body," his voice stuttering, still fixated on the swaying torso banging on the trunk with a sickening thud. On arrival the police cut the body down and started searching for any identification, sifting through the pockets. They came across a wallet containing a fat wad of cash, a drivers licence plus other items of no real relevance. The name Zack Graham was the name etched on to the licence. The police also found a hand-written note in the inner coat pocket, saying about drug deals and who was involved, and a confession to the murder of a friend. The note stated that Zack could not live with himself through this, even though in his mind it needed to be done. The police now had names with which to carry out an investigation. And sure enough, the press soon got hold of it.

Jim again woke with a banging hangover. The mood of the day was extremely grim, with the rain coursing down the window. He stared out into the gloom as cars going by splashed through puddles built up through the night. Some early risers were out for a morning jog.

"How the fuck can you get up at stupid o'clock on a Sunday to go jogging?"

The thought totally bewildered Jim as he sank back into his bed. He could smell the dankness of the previous night's escapades. He flicked on the TV in his room. A reporter from the East Midlands news was talking about a body that had been found in their home town. Evidence of a suspected suicide linked to a murder and a major drug ring had been established through a letter found on the body. When they read the name of the victim, Jim sat up, and his hangover automatically subsided.

"Fucking hell!"

Jim yelled, for he knew exactly who they were talking about. Tom came in to see what he was shouting about.

"I just flicked on the news and there's a story about a suicide, murder and drug dealers back home."

The look of surprise shone across Jim's face. Tom looked at Jim.

"Okay, there was, but what was all the shouting about?"

"Well, they just read out the name of the suicide victim. They say a note was found on him but they haven't released any more names, just the details of what was in the note. But the suicide guy they found was Zack."

Tom's eyes widened.

"That drug dealer guy who was mates with that Daz was a bit quiet, not like that mouthy shit. Well, it looks like he got more than he could handle."

If Tom had any sort of sympathy he didn't outwardly show it. Jim nodded, scratching his head.

"Well, Daz did tell me they were getting involved with some major people with the cocaine and that, so I'm guessing it was all tied together."

"Well, you get what you deserve if you start messing around with those types. Well, obviously things didn't go to plan for this to happen," Tom said, walking off swigging his tea. Will was told about the events that had taken place. He just shrugged his shoulders.

"Oh well, what do you expect?"

Jim kept an eye on the news all that day. More things started to emerge about what had happened. The police had released all the details about what was written on that note, that he had shot his friend, who was only known as Daz, plus various other names who were known to the police that were involved with the smuggling of drugs and the gangland murder. The reporter stated that arrest warrants had been issued for the people named on that letter.

"Wow, that's some crazy shit," Jim said, still stunned by what happened and more to the point, they knew them. The recovery process was now back on from the previous night. Jim had sunk back into his hangover after the shock news had temporarily eased the suffering.

They met Charlie and Quinney at the venue. Drinks were again in full swing and the discussion turned to what had happened back at home.

Charlie just said, "You don't fuck around with those sorts of people; it's just not wise."

He told them a story of a similar incident back in the seventies where it got very messy. He too had been involved with those types, and nothing good ever came out of it; he got out while he could. Jim's phone buzzed. It was Katrina. She said she would be down on the Wednesday. She sounded quite distant, like her mind was elsewhere. Jim was pleased just to hear her voice – he had missed her so much – and he asked if she was okay, and whether she was getting morning sickness. He apologised for not calling. He said the schedule was hectic. He didn't let her know he was always too hungover to call. She said it was fine. Jim again sensed there was something wrong.

"Is everything okay? Is there anything you want to tell me?"

Katrina got quite irate.

"No, I'm fine. I will see you Wednesday, okay!"

Jim was taken aback by her sudden mood swing. "Okay, well, I love –"

The phone cut off. Jim's paranoia kicked in. Why didn't she say she loved him, why was she so distant, and a whole bunch of other questions kept running through his head. He finally put it down to the pregnancy; it must be taking it out of her. He had to have something to ease his mind for the gig later, but it didn't quite work, for the show was not on a par with the other one. Jim's focus was on Katrina. He kept it quiet; he didn't want to bother the others with his problems. Both Tom and Will asked Jim afterwards why he was off. Jim just said he didn't feel that great, but still the crowd were not put off by this and they let the band know when they came off, to their surprise. But Jim felt he had put on a poor show. And although they seemed to have enjoyed it, Jim apologised to all the people he spoke with after, including Charlie and Quinney, and he said he hoped it wouldn't affect their recording sessions. They were both understanding. "No, course it won't," Quinney reassured Jim.

Chapter 25

Monday came around, and the excitement was overwhelming. They couldn't believe they were going into a proper studio to record. Jim was feeling good, a lot better than the day before. He thought about Katrina and how she spoke and just put it down to tiredness with the pregnancy.

"Well, it's gotta take it out of you," he thought.

Charlie was there bright and early to pick them up and take them down to the studio.

"Good morning, my fine little rock stars," Charlie said with a sly wink and full-on cockney charm.

They all just looked at each other as if to say, "What the fuck?"

The journey took about half an hour. It would've taken much longer through the London traffic, but old Charlie was clued up on all the back roads to cut it out. They pulled up outside the studio, and stepped out of the car as the sun was breaking through the morning fog.

"Here you go, lads, your studio awaits," Charlie said in the style of those horse-drawn carriage guys saying, "Your carriage awaits."

His arm was swaying towards the front gates. The studio was an old Victorian-style house, with large front windows and a solid front door, traditional for the style of that period. Once inside Charlie took them down a long hallway, which felt too long for the house, kind of a Tardis from *Dr Who*: small on the outside but big inside. They heard the sound of drums echoing through, which excited Tom. When they reached the end of the hallway, where the sound was coming from, they entered a big room. All the amps were set up in the corners, and a drum kit was set back in the centre of the room, where a guy was playing. Tom stopped to watch and then caught up with the others. This room turned out to be a rehearsal room.

They followed on through up to a flight of stairs, reminiscent of something out of a manor house, set in the centre of the hall. Another hall ran beyond the rear of the staircase.

"This place seems to go on forever," Will quipped.

"Nearly there," Charlie said.

"Hello, guys." A voice came from above. It was Quinney leaning over the banister.

"Well, I'm glad you made it all right and didn't get lost." He smirked at Charlie.

Charlie just shook head. "Right, I'll leave you in his capable hands, I guess."

He then returned the same expression. Quinney replied with a courteous middle finger. "Right, lads, I'll give you the grand tour of the upper floor."

While walking round, they asked Quinney all sorts of questions. They wanted to get as much information as possible, which Quinney was more than happy to provide.

And after that, Quinney put the kettle on; he always started a session with a tea and a smoke. Jim and Will set their instruments down to start re-tuning them, since the journey there hadn't exactly been smooth, while Tom set himself on the drums. It was the nicest drum kit he had played on, and he said so.

"Fuck me, this kit is proper shit hot!" Tom said, kind of forgetting where he was. "Oh, sorry," he said, feeling slightly embarrassed.

Quinney just laughed and retorted with a hint of sarcasm, "Well, I'm glad it meets with your approval."

Jim set out the song list, even though everyone knew the running order. Quinney rolled up a few spliffs.

"I do take it you partake?"

All replied with a solid, "Yes."

They were all getting nice and stoned before the session. Quinney burnt some incense; he liked that whole hippyish vibe, as he thought it made everyone relax. There were no complaints from the lads, except Will, who was not keen on the joss sticks – he thought they smelled horrible.

Katrina had just got into Euston station. She felt relieved to get down there, away from what was happening in her life back home, or what she thought was left back at home. She tried calling Jim on his mobile but there was no answer. She made her way down to the Thames, looking out onto the water, reliving the previous few days. She felt physically sick but was relieved to be out of the way.

Back at the studio the recording was moving along nicely. They were all good and stoned while listening to the playbacks.

"Bit shoddy in places, but for a first recording, it wasn't too bad," Quinney said.

"Well, lads, we've got some pretty good songs down. This is only demo form; I just wanted you guys to get used to everything, but you're doing well."

The day had gone so quickly that when they left it was dark. Quinney took them round the corner for a few beers, which no one complained about. While Quinney brought the first round over, he told them about a party which was being held over in Hammersmith the following weekend: they were very welcome to come.

"There will be some very exciting people there, people in the know who could really take you places."

They were all ears; the excitement, as well as the dope and booze, was flowing through their systems.

"I mean, Charlie's a great guy and that and is most certainly a top bloke to know if you're looking for gigs down here, but now I'm talking some serious people. Get your foot in the door with these guys, and you know the old saying," he said while sitting back taking a swig from his whiskey. Jim and the others sat there with blank faces.

"No, what saying?" Tom said, slurring his words.

Quinney frowned. "You know, 'The sky's the limit'."

They still sat there, stone-faced, not knowing about that saying.

"So, who said that then?" Will said, still none the wiser.

Quinney blew out his cheeks.

"Fuck me, you boys are hard work," he said and laughed. "Well, I don't know who coined the phrase, but it is a saying."

Jim then said, "Right-oh, well, whose round is it?" without giving that conversation a second thought.

Katrina was still wandering the streets, her mind plagued, finally making her way over to where Jim was staying. Jim had left the address for her before he left. She was waiting on the steps by the time they got back a couple of hours later.

"Oi, Jim, wake up. Is that your bird from back home?" Charlie said.

Jim woke up, all bleary-eyed. They had all fallen sleep in the back of Charlie's car after the drinking session with Quinney. Rubbing his eyes, he stared out of the window.

"Yeah, that's her. She said she was coming down. What's she doing sitting there?"

"Waiting for you, I'm guessing," Charlie said.

"Yeah, but at this time?" Jim replied.

They pulled up to the curb, and Jim got out first. "Hello, Katrina. What are you doing here? It's a bit late; I would've thought you would get down earlier."

Katrina went over to him and gave him a big hug. "I tried calling, but I take it your phone was switched off. I've missed you," she said and kissed him.

Jim explained they had been recording all day then went out with the producer after for a few drinks and that he hadn't been on his phone all night. A crack of thunder rolled over the night sky followed by a streak of lightning. This freaked Katrina out; she didn't like this kind of weather. They made their way inside as the rain started to come down hard. The other two came in soaked, even though they had only walked the short distance. They greeted Katrina, asked her how she was doing, and left them to it. Jim offered Katrina a drink from the numerous bottles of spirits Charlie had supplied the flat with. She opted for vodka orange.

Jim then realised. "Oh shit – you can't drink while you're pregnant."

"Well, one won't hurt," she said.

Jim staggered back with the drinks and told Katrina all about the recording sessions they had done that day, and he asked her about her journey. She was very quiet and vague in her answers.

"So how's it been? When did you find out you were pregnant?"

"Oh, Jim, I'm tired. Can we discuss this another time?"

Jim accepted that Katrina must be exhausted from all that traveling and wandering round all day. He showed her to his room and said she could stay there and that he would sleep on the sofa. Jim felt awkward about sleeping together after the way she had spoken to him on the phone, as he thought they had broken up, even though she wanted him to stay with her.

But he made the point that it was best they slept apart. The next day Katrina came in the room totally different from the previous night, more talkative, but she didn't bring up the previous night's conversation.

Jim didn't say anything about it either, as he thought it would create unnecessary tension.

They went out for breakfast and then went to see the sights together, on the London Eye, etcetera. They were getting along just fine. But Jim still sensed something underlying was wrong, like Katrina was holding something back. Katrina stayed at the flat when they went to record that evening and had a gig the next night. She seemed very excited about seeing them play again.

"It's been a while since I last saw you guys play; I'm looking forward to it," she told Will.

"Yeah. Hopefully we'll put on a good show for you," Jim said.

Jim didn't know if he was being paranoid or not, but it seemed to him that Katrina was keeping her distance from him, for whatever reason. Every time he went to her she made a beeline for either Will or Tom and would start some random conversation. It made them quite uncomfortable, as they saw what she was doing and knew something wasn't quite right. On the way to the studio Jim asked them if they thought she was acting strange.

Will shrugged. "Yeah, but I didn't want to say anything in front of her."

Tom was in agreement and asked Jim if Katrina had said anything out of the ordinary.

Jim shook his head.

"Not really. We had quite a good time today, but at times she was pretty distant, like she was in deep thought, but I just thought that was me being paranoid." Jim left all that at the door when they got to the studio; he didn't want any negative thoughts to fuck anything up. The session went really well and they got a lot done. Again they went round the corner for post-session drinks, which would become their new ritual, to wind down and discuss all that they had got done. Jim called Katrina, but her phone went straight to answer phone. Jim again started to feel a desperation. His paranoia came back. He made an excuse and headed for the toilet.

Jim needed some breathing time to relax, so he lit up a spliff and sat with his head in his hands. He had gone there to get away from all the shit back there. He thought it was just following him, so he decided to have it out with Katrina and find out what was going on. When he got back to the table, he told Tom and Will what he was going to do. Quinney disagreed. He was brought up to scratch with the whole situation.

"Don't ask her yet. She might do a runner and end up god knows where. Just leave it for the time being and let her settle down; I'm sure she'll tell you everything in good time." Quinney then went to get another round. He again complimented the boys on the session and said that they were getting some good stuff down. They got back to the flat around two-ish. Jim went to check on Katrina; she was still asleep in his room. He noticed that her eyes were red and blotchy, like she'd been crying. Her phone was on the side, and it still had text messages up on the screen that she had been received. Jim didn't want to pry into her private conversations, but he noticed the messages were from her ex, the guy Jim had had a fight with. This sent Jim's paranoia into overdrive. He left it at that, as he didn't want to know what it was, even though in the back of his mind the curiosity was overwhelming.

Jim went back into the kitchen and grabbed a beer out of the fridge. He pressed the cold can against his face then opened it and took a big swig. He really wished he hadn't looked at Katrina's phone. A whole host of scenarios was running through his head. Lying in the darkness, Jim felt the walls closing in, as if his mind wasn't fucked enough. He soon drifted off.

Chapter 26

Jim awoke the next morning with a cold, wet feeling on his legs. He had fallen asleep with a can still in his hand, which was now tipped up over him.

"Oh, shit," Jim said as he sat up. The coldness of the room had made his clothes even more uncomfortable. The thoughts of the previous night came flooding back. He held his head in his hands, rubbing his temples in a circular motion, trying to shake the feeling. He had no more tablets; he needed to stabilise, as this was driving him mad. The only thing he could do was self-medicate, which in turn would drive him more over the edge. He took a shower to try and wash away all the excesses in body and mind. Feeling slightly better and with some fresh clothes on, Jim went to make his morning coffee when his phone buzzed. He answered, and it was Terry seeing how everything was going.

"Yeah, fine, Terry. The SG is sounding great. Thanks again for that, Terry."

Terry was calling to let Jim know that he was coming down for their next gig and also to see how the recording was going, as he wanted to hear what they had down.

"Well, I could send you some on your email," Jim said.

"No; I haves shut up the shops for a few days, so I am coming downs today for tonight's gig and I will listen to your stuff next time yous are in the studios. There's nothing like listening to new tracks in a studio."

"Cool. I will see you when you get down then," Jim said.

When the others finally emerged, Jim told them about Terry coming down.

"That'll be cool. Do you think now that we know each other quite well, he would get me some more drum sticks at mate's rates?" Tom said.

Jim shook his head. "You are unbelievable."

At that, Will punched Tom in the arm. "Shut up, you clown." Tom just shrugged. "What?"

Katrina came in. Her face was very sullen. "Jim, I need to tell you something. Can we go and talk in private?"

This made Jim very nervous. He hated those downbeat I-need-to-tell-you-something conversations, as nothing good could come from them. With trepidation he asked Will and Tom if they could make themselves scarce for a while. They agreed, Tom saying to Will they should go out for breakfast.

Once they were out of the door, Katrina went in to the kitchen to fix Jim and herself a drink, and when she came back in holding two glasses of neat double Jack Daniel's, Jim looked at the glasses.

"Wow; that's certainly an early start. This can't be good."

Jim was trying to make light of the deep conversation he knew was going to be held. He took the glass and sat down on the sofa. Katrina stood looking out of the window with a thousand-yard stare. She took a large sip from her glass. A single tear streamed down her right cheek.

"Jim, I've got some things to tell you. It's not going to be easy for me telling you and it's going to be equally unpleasant for you."

Jim downed his drink in one, lit a cigarette, went over to where the drinks were and poured himself another. Katrina raised her glass for another, as she had finished hers. Her hand was shaking as he poured the dark brown liquid. It seemed to take an eternity for the glass to fill. Jim again sat down.

"Okay, well, I've known something was wrong by the way you have been acting and the phone calls, plus ever since you got down here, the atmosphere has been kind of tense, but I'm sure we can work something out, whatever it is," Jim said, shrugging.

"I'm pregnant, Jim."

"I know that; you already told me," Jim said with a hint of sarcasm.

Katrina just stared at Jim. More tears started to roll down her face as she took another drink.

"You are going to really hate me." Her voice was wobbling with each word.

"Okay, what is it? Just say it," Jim said, again shrugging, trying to keep his composure. Inside his anxiety levels were fit to bursting; his hands were also shaking.

"I'm sorry, Jim, but but the baby's not yours."

Jim's entire world froze, like time had stood still. He felt the trapdoor flung open beneath him as the words came pouring out, the noose tightening round his neck, feeling like he couldn't breathe.

"What!"

Jim's voice quivered. A gut-wrenching feeling took over. He fell from the sofa onto his knees, trying in that instant to comprehend what Katrina had said.

"Please, say something, Jim," Katrina said, pleading with him.

Jim, now facing the floor, shook his head, rubbing his hands through his hair then grabbing it. "What the fuck do you expect me to say? Oh, congratulations on your baby that should've been fucking mine!"

Jim was Seething. He couldn't believe what he was being told. He managed to sit back on the sofa, his head still in his hands.

"Okay, well, whose is it then?"

His face was red; tears were streaming down it. Katrina sat down on the sofa, holding her glass with both hands, her head bowed. She took a few shaky, deep breaths and another sip of her drink.

"Well, you know that time at the pub when you had a go at those guys for talking to me? Well, when I left in the taxi, I went on to another pub, just to try and calm down."

Her voice quivered, as she was trying to hold it together.

"I was there just having a quiet drink, when my ex came in; you know, that guy you had the fight with."

Jim raised his head, his eyes narrowed, gritting his teeth. His lips were quivering, for he knew what the outcome was going to be.

"We just got talking. I told him he was a twat for starting that fight with you, and then I said about how you were acting that night, with those other guys."

Jim got up and poured himself a larger glass of Jack Daniel's. He lit another cigarette, fell back against the wall and slid down so he was sitting with his knees raised, his cold stare piercing straight through her. Katrina continued.

"I started to cry, as I felt I just got the idiots for boyfriends. Everyone else seemed to be with decent blokes, and I got the rejects."

Jim half-smiled. "Thanks for calling me a reject."

Katrina glared at him. "Fuck off, Jim, if you can't be serious about this."

Jim shook his head. "I am serious! You fuck another guy and get yourself knocked up, and you're trying to tell me what to do!" He laughed.

"Well, we had a few more drinks. I didn't want to be alone, so we went back to mine, and one thing led –" she paused. "It was just that once, I promise," she said quickly, just to get the whole thing out without any more going round the houses.

"Well, I thought you were on the pill, which made me a bit surprised when you said you were pregnant, but I never questioned it, as it still can happen."

"I was on the pill, but I might have forgotten to take it that day; I don't know," Katrina said.

"How convenient. Seems like you wanted his kid all along."

Jim blew out his cheeks. He couldn't think at all; his mind was spiralling even worse this time. He didn't have his medication to fall back on and the alcohol was now taking effect. Jim said, "I cannot stay here. I've gotta get out."

When Will and Tom arrived back, they found Katrina sitting alone on the sofa, drunk, with the bottle of Jack Daniel's in her hand, tears rolling down her face.

"Hello, Katrina. Where's Jim gone?" Will said, taking the bottle off her.

Katrina remained silent.

"A bit early for that, isn't it?" he said. "Everything okay with you two?" He sat down next to her.

"No; everything is far from okay with us two. It's my entire fault."

Tom then came in. "What's happened here? Somebody die?" He laughed.

"No, but I wish I was dead," Katrina said.

Tom's face dropped, as if he had said something wrong, but obviously he and Will didn't know what had gone on. He also made a similar remark to Will's about Katrina drinking so early.

Katrina started to explain everything to them about what had happened, about Jim's behaviour which had led to things always going wrong, also about the baby not being his and that she had gone off with an ex because of Jim's behaviour. Will interpreted it as her shifting the blame.

"Well, we know Jim can be a pain in the arse, and he can also be very erratic, especially when he's been on something, but –" Will paused to choose the right words. "But he didn't deserve this. I mean, what the fuck were you thinking?"

Katrina started to cry again, thinking about the whole mess.

"Well, where's he gone now?" Tom then said.

Katrina just shook her head and shrugged.

Will then said, "We best go look for him; you never know what he's gonna do."

He then turned to Katrina.

"And I also think you best get your stuff and get out of here. We can't have this."

"Well, where am I supposed to go?" Katrina looked shocked by what Will had said.

"You could always go to a hotel, go back home or stay with that other guy, for all I care. It seems you didn't think about Jim when you shagged him. "Tom said

Tom and Will got their coats back on and headed out but not before Will turned to Katrina. "If he's done something stupid then it's all on you."

Katrina heard the front door slam. She lit a cigarette and reclined back on the sofa, thinking about the whole mess.

Chapter 27

The day was shifting into gear as Jim ambled along the streets, looking for a bar that was open, looking at all the people milling about, heading to their places of work, and thinking about the day ahead. Jim passed into obscurity, with no one paying him any mind, oblivious to his dejection. He just needed to rid himself of the thoughts tearing into his psyche and edging him back into the darkness.

He found a bar where he could sit for a while. All the shit was running around in his head along with the withdrawals from his medication. His head was buzzing and waving with every movement. Those lurking problems were arising once more; that black hood was again shrouding him as anxiety set him on edge.

He ordered a beer plus a whiskey and took them up to the end of the bar. He lit a cigarette. The barman told him to go outside to smoke, so he put the fag out on the bar, unbeknown to barman, who by this time was facing the other direction. Jim downed each drink and moved on. He tripped up on some uneven paving, for he wasn't looking where he was going. He was just staring out into the bleakness of life, caring not where he would end up, losing all sense of what was real. His reality was dimming fast, and he couldn't get to grips with anything. The shock was too great. The sky was over-cast. Spots of rain started to fall on Jim. He enjoyed the freshness of the rain and cool air, but the low-lying clouds were making him very heady.

Will and Tom made their way down to where they thought Jim would go: the row of bars a couple of streets away from where they were staying, plus they tried his mobile, which was switched off, but they kept trying anyway. They went into each bar that was open, asking if they had seen Jim, but no one had.

As Jim picked up a bottle of bourbon from a supermarket, the girl on the till looked wearily at the dishevelled sight fumbling for his money, change dropping from his pockets. Finally pulling a twenty, he threw it on the side and went without collecting his change or picking up the money he had dropped. The checkout girl shouted after him but he just ignored her. Swigging from the bottle, Jim made his way down to the river, just to be away from everyone. He couldn't face people with that humiliation hanging over him, feeling that everybody knew his situation. Jim just wanted to score really badly, as he hadn't touched anything since being down there, except a bit of weed. Numbing that pain was everything. He clocked a couple of guys who he thought looked like dealers so tried his luck and got a result. They asked Jim what his name was and where he was from. Jim told them in a vague manner that he was from the East Midlands. He also said about the band, the gigs and the recording sessions they were down for.

They were deeply impressed. "So you're living the rock 'n' roll lifestyle?"

Jim laughed. "Well, yeah, kind of, but without all the money."

They introduced themselves as Roach and Kel.

"So why do they call you Roach?" Jim asked.

Kel replied for him. "Because he smokes so much weed." He laughed.

Roach didn't say much, but he laughed along. Jim was putting a brave face on it, but still he didn't give a shit. He just wanted to numb the pain in any way possible. He had a feeling he could get mugged at any time, but he just kept swigging on his bottle. Roach noticed him drinking and commented on how it was too early to be drinking that stuff.

Jim didn't take any notice. Roach glanced over at Kel, who just shrugged.

Roach and Kel took Jim over the other side of the river to a flat on an estate. They went inside, leaving Jim on the doorstep. A few minutes later, they came back out and said he was good to go.

"Okay, mate, you can come in." Jim followed them through.

Inside, the house was not the epitome of cleanliness, but it wasn't too bad compared to the places he had seen on those documentaries when the police raided those crack houses. Jim pulled out fifty pounds he had taken from the supply tin Charlie had left.

"Right, what the fuck can I get with this?"

Jim was pretty loaded now after drinking for most of the morning. He sat down on a long leather couch. People were coming in and out of the room. Wads of cash were tucked under the glass table, and bags of weed were on top. A heavy-set guy came out, his arms plastered with tattoos, gold rings on each of his fingers. He sat down in front of Jim, shook his hand and smiled. He was smoking a blunt. He kept licking his lips after every drag. Smoke bellowed from the end. The guy did not say a word. He reached over, pulled out a bag of coke from a cupboard drawer and drew up a few lines.

"Here you go, mate; on the house." He felt sorry for Jim and the state he was in.

Then Kel nodded towards the money Jim had laid out. He reached out to grab it but the other guy lent forward and got him round the neck, his big hands crushing down on Kel's windpipe.

"You little fucker; that's not how to do business."

As he let go, Kel fell to the floor holding his neck, gasping for breath. It seemed this guy was the main man in the house. He watched as Jim hoovered up all the lines, after which he came alive. The guy introduced himself as Wes and again shook Jim's hand as Jim introduced himself.

"You look like you've had a bit of a shitty morning."

Jim looked up at him, all glazed. "You don't know the fucking half of it."

Jim then said, "So now you have my money, I'll have a couple more grams of that charlie. Anything else in stock?"

Jim took a swig from the bottle.

"Get this man a fucking glass," the guy told one of the other guys.

When the guy came back with the glass, Jim poured a large drink and put the bottle on the table.

"Right, come with me."

Wes took Jim into a back room, where a number of people were sitting on huge cushions, completely out of it, like zombies. Jim was on the other end of the spectrum, all coked up.

"So have you ever tried heroin?" Wes asked.

"Well, nope, but I am game. Fuck it!"

"Well, take a seat."

Wes went to the corner of the room, where there was a large table. He brought over some foil and a paper wrap containing some brown powder. He tipped the powder onto the foil. Jim grabbed hold of it and took out his lighter.

"Well, I have seen this done before," Jim said with a big, glazed smile.

Wes then handed Jim a straw to smoke it. Jim inhaled the smoke rising from the foil. It seemed Wes must have forgotten or didn't care that Jim had done a load of coke.

Just the money was important. Jim lay back feeling, the effects, a big smile etched across his face. His features then changed. His eyes rolled back into his head and he started to convulse, shaking uncontrollably, saliva foaming from his mouth.

"Oh, fuck, man!" Wes shouted.

Both Kel and Roach came in. "What's up, man?"

"It's him. I think he's OD-ing. We gotta get him the fuck of here."

They grabbed Jim, picked him up and dragged him to a back door which led to a fire escape, making sure no one was around. They pulled him down the stairs, threw him into the back of a car and sped off.

Chapter 28

Will and Tom were still searching. There was no sign of Jim anywhere, and his phone was now going straight to voice mail.

"For fuck's sake; where can he be?" Tom questioned.

Will then called up Charlie and let him know the situation. Charlie told them to stay put and that he'd be down as soon as possible. Katrina had followed them down. She went up to them.

"Any luck?"

"Well, does it fucking look like it!" Will said. "I thought we told you to do one."

"I feel so guilty. I need to do something to help find him," Katrina said as the waterworks resumed.

"Well, don't you think you've done enough?" Tom said, equally as pissed off with her.

A few minutes later Charlie turned up with Terry, who had just arrived in London. They all got in the car to start the search. They looked in every conceivable place they thought Jim might go. Will then thought he might go out looking for drugs, which he told Charlie.

"Right. I'm gonna make a few calls to some people who might know if he has."

Charlie knew some of the more unsavoury characters around London who had contacts with every dealer in and around the London area.

Kel and Roach were still ferrying Jim's convulsive body around, searching for a place to get rid of him. They were panicked about being caught with him.

"For fuck's sake, what shall we do with him?" Kel said.

Roach was concentrating on the road, trying not to draw attention to them. Jim was moaning in the back, falling in and out of consciousness. Kel kept on looking round, staring at Jim; he began feeling a huge sense of guilt. Usually he didn't give a fuck, but there was something about Jim he liked.

"Hey, man, we've gotta get him to a hospital; this isn't right," Kel said.

"Are you fucking crazy, man? We drop him at a hospital, we're both done for."

Kel said, "No; I need to do it."

"Well then, you're on your own. I don't want any part of it; I just wanna get rid, soon as."

Kel said, "Fucking hell, ain't you got a conscience?"

Roach shook his head then stopped the car. "Right, get out and take him; the hospital's just down there."

Kel got out and then got Jim out, who was more or less lifeless.

"You really gonna fuck off and leave us?" Kel said, lifting Jim.

Roach just grabbed the door then sped off without saying a word. Kel wrapped one of Jim's arms around his neck for support, like a soldier dragging an injured comrade from the battlefield. Jim was like a dead weight. Kel struggled as Jim dragged his feet; Kel was not the biggest of people. When they finally reached the hospital, Kel let Jim slump into one of the seats in the reception and called out for somebody to help. A nurse was walking down towards them. Kel grabbed her and dragged her over to where Jim was sitting.

The nurse lifted Jim's head. He was now turning blue, so she radioed a crash team down to reception. The nurse asked if Jim had taken anything. Kel didn't say a word and ran off.

Soon the team arrived and loaded Jim onto a stretcher, working on him, as his breathing was laboured, and loosening his upper clothes, checking the airwaves and applying an oxygen mask. They then took him to the emergency area.

Charlie had no luck with his contacts. Will and Tom were in a deep state of panic, desperate for their friend to come back. Katrina sat there, not saying a word, just sobbing. Will looked over at her, shaking his head.

"I'm truly sorry for all this shit I've caused; I didn't mean to hurt him." Katrina's voice was quivering. Tom said in a low voice, "I suggest you shut the fuck up. You've caused enough damage for one day."

"All rights, all this negativity is gettings us nowhere. We just need to finds him," Terry said. Just then Charlie's phone rang. It was the hospital, letting him know that they had found his number in Jim's wallet and asking if he knew the patient. Charlie said that he did.

"So what's happened to him? Is he okay?" Charlie asked.

"We cannot say too much at the minute, but we just thought we'd let you know," the nurse responded. They headed straight to the hospital. The nurse who first dealt with the situation was at reception. Will ran up to her, asking where Jim was and if he was okay. She took them into a side room and explained that someone had brought Jim in and then run off. They were running toxicology tests and would have to wait for the results.

"We've got him in intensive care," the nurse informed them, "so if you call back tomorrow, you might be able to see him. We suspect a drug overdose."

"I knew it! I fucking knew it!" Tom shouted. "This is all down on you," he said, venting his anger towards Katrina, who just sat there, deeply shaken by what had just been said.

Charlie then suggested they all go back home to calm down and come back the next day.

Katrina then said, "Is it okay to stay tonight, so I can come back tomorrow?"

Will exploded. "You've got some fucking front asking that. I suggest you get the next train back home, and we'll send you your clothes back."

Terry said, "Come on, nows, all this is doings nobody any good. I'm staying at a Travelodge nearby; I'll gets you a room there; gives everybody a bits of breathing space." That was all settled. Charlie then drove everyone back to their respective places. It was a long night for everybody. They didn't know whether Jim would live or die.

The next morning Will and Tom woke especially early. They wanted to get down the hospital soon as possible. They called Charlie and asked whether they could get a lift. They had found that Jim had not only taken the fifty pounds but all the money from their supply tin. They let Charlie know.

"Okay, lads, give me an hour and I will be right with you."

Tom started drinking early. He couldn't handle what was going on; it was all like a bad dream. Will grabbed the can out of his hand and threw it against the wall.

"For fuck's sake, Tom, we've gotta keep it together!"

Tom sat down. His whole body was trembling; he couldn't focus.

"What if he dies?" Tom said, the words stuttering.

Will sat down with him and put his arm round him.

"Come on, man, he's not gonna die. That idiot is made of much sterner stuff than the rest of us."

Will knew how hollow those words were, but he had to say something to try and keep it together. Just then the doorbell rang. It was Charlie and Terry. Will buzzed them up.

"All right, lads? You ready?" Charlie noticed the look on Tom's face. "You okay, mate?" Charlie said.

He then pulled Will to one side. "If it's too much for him, I'll stay with him, and you can go with Terry to go see him."

Will then asked where Katrina was.

"She's in the car. You know, she's still very distraught."

Charlie had a very concerned look on his face, as if to say, she might do something stupid. Will then asked Tom if he was okay to go. He knew he wasn't but just asked out of politeness. He didn't want to go without saying anything. Tom sat there. He didn't really acknowledge what was said. He waved his arm as if to say, just leave me.

Charlie then said, "You guys go; let me know how it goes." He pulled out a wad of notes and stuffed some into Will's hand and some back into the tin, from which Jim had released the other funds. When down at the car, Will saw Katrina in the back seat. He got in the front and didn't say one word to her.

"Good morning, Will," Katrina said, her voice still broken.

Will casually nodded but didn't say a word.

"Is Tom not coming?" she asked.

Will turned around. "Look, just cause we're going to the same place, doesn't mean I've gotta talk to you."

Katrina then lit up a cigarette. Will was not amused and said so.

"Just because the kid's not Jim's, it still deserves a chance. Fucking smoking while you're pregnant – that is fucking bang out of order. You can go ahead and kill yourself if you want, but don't take it out of the kid!"

Will then grabbed the cigarette out of her hand and threw it out of the window.

"Come ons, people," Terry said. "Cans we just gets along, for Jim's sake?"

The rest of the journey was masked in an uncomfortable silence. When they arrived at the hospital, Terry went up to the reception desk.

"Hello, coulds you tell us the room Jim Staley is stayings in?"

The nurse searched on the computer.

"Yes; he's on ward twenty-eight, up on the fourth floor."

They headed up. Still, Will had no time for Katrina. He felt she was feeling sorry for herself rather than having any consideration for Jim. When they reached the ward, they had to ring the bell to be let in. A nurse came down and asked who they were there to see, and she led them to where Jim was. They came to a side room, where the curtains were open. Will peered through the window and saw Jim lying there, a tube down his throat helping him breathe. The nurse asked them not to make too much noise whilst in there. Katrina went straight over to Jim and gave him a kiss, whispering that she was sorry for everything and asking if he could find any way to forgive her. Will heard what she said.

"I cannot believe what I'm hearing; now you want forgiveness?"

Terry then said, "How's about we's take it in turns to sits with him? All this animosity is doings everyone's no good."

They both agreed.

"Well, I'm staying with him first," Katrina said.

Will scowled at her for that domineering tone, "Oh, right, so you're taking control of the situation which you caused? Says it all, really." He shook his head while heading out of the door.

"Terry, let me know when she's gone. I'm going to get a coffee; do you want one?"

Terry smiled. "I'm okay, thanks, but I will lets you know when she's done."

Terry then shut the door. He waited outside while Katrina was in there. Katrina looked at Jim then made sure Terry was outside.

"Oh, thanks a lot, you fucking selfish prick," she said. "Now I'm getting all this shit all because YOU couldn't keep it together."

Will was in the cafeteria. He called up Tom to see how he was doing. He was surprised when Charlie answered.

"Hello, Charlie. How's Tom doing?"

"He's okay; just sleeping at the minute. He snuck some booze into his room and has passed out. I went in to check on him, because he was gone for a while. I found a few beer cans and a bottle of vodka on the floor."

"Oh, fucking hell; I don't need him messing up as well. I cannot be doing with two fuck ups." Charlie laughed. "No, I don't think he's messing up. He's just not dealing with this situation very well."

Charlie went on to ask how Jim was doing and whether it was okay with Katrina being there, and also if Terry was okay. Will replied, "That fucking Kat! She has totally dominated the situation, saying that she would see him first and that. She's really winding me up. I can't wait for her to leave."

Charlie paused for a second. "Oh, right; not going too well then?"

"Nope, not by a long shot. Anyway, I gotta go. I think Terry's trying to get through."

Terry told Will that Katrina had done and he could come back now. This really pissed Will off. He thought, "Oh, I can come back now?" It grated on him that she was controlling when everyone could see Jim. When Will got back to the ward, he had to bite his tongue when he saw Katrina sitting there. He didn't want to make another scene, so he stepped into the room, just looking at Jim. A tear streamed down his face.

"Fucking hell, mate, why did you do this? We could've worked it out another way. Anyway," Will said, wiping his face, "Tom sends his best, and Charlie. Tom's back at the flat, completely off his tits." Will laughed. "Well, mate, I will come back with him when he sobers up. He doesn't know how to deal with this. Take it easy, mate."

After Will came out, Terry poked his head through the door and said, "Takes it easy, Jim. We'll be backs tomorrow."

Chapter 29

The lights were extremely blurry as Jim opened his eyes. He couldn't move any part of his body. His eyes circled round the room. He was confused about where he was. The beeping noises from the machines were buzzing in his ears.

"Where the hell am I?" he thought. Even though his mind was still very mixed up, he could still ask these rhetorical questions. A nurse entered the room. She checked his information, located on a board on the end of his bed, and also messed around with his drip, making sure there was enough fluid in there. As she left, Jim noticed a man standing in the doorway. He looked quite familiar but Jim couldn't quite work out who it was.

"Hello, Jim. It's been a while. Well, I didn't expect to see you here, but I saw your name on the patient list so thought I'd pay a visit."

Even though Jim was in this state, he worked out who it was. It was Dan, from his old work place.

"Out of all the fucking people to see me like this, it had to be him," Jim thought.

Jim tried to speak but the tube was preventing that, he fiddled with the tube, then pointed out the door towards where the nurses were. Dan got what Jim was trying to say, he then went out and came back with a nurse. She saw that Jim was conscious and went back out to get a doctor, who came in checked on Jim and decided it was okay to remove the tube. The doctor asked Dan to leave until they were done. When they had finished with everything and left, Dan came back in and sat down.

"So what happened to you then, Jim?" Dan asked.

Jim, still very weak, shrugged. "One minute I was round this house, the next, I'm in here."

"Well, you look like shit, mate," Dan said with an air of arrogance as he flicked back his hair. Jim raised his eyebrows. It sent a cold chill down his back that this guy would call him mate.

"Anyway, I'm here to see a relative, who's just over in that next ward, then I'm going round to see the sights," Dan said while swigging on his coffee. "Oh yeah, you wouldn't have heard, but old Mr Osborne checked out last week. Lung cancer, all those cigars. I knew it would happen. Right, gotta go. No hard feelings, hey?" he said, reaching out his hand. Jim just stared at him, unable to move. Also, he didn't have the energy or the patience to converse any more. Dan laughed. "Don't get up. I'll see myself out. Oh, by the way, I didn't call the police. I wasn't going to; I just thought I'd let you sweat." He smirked and then left.

Jim thought, "Still a fucking moron."

Jim looked out of the window at the trees blowing in the breeze, trying to recollect everything that had happened.

"How the hell did I get here?"

The confusion rattled his fragile mind.

Will told Terry he would get a taxi back to the flat. Katrina had done a disappearing act when she was done with the visit. They couldn't find her when they were ready to leave. Will didn't care one way or another whether they found her or not. Terry had also made his own way back, as he said he needed the space to think. While travelling on the tube, as he had left the car in the car park, Terry contacted Jim's folks to let them know what had happened. He texted Charlie to let him know where his car was. Jim's mum was the one to answer the call from Terry. She completely freaked out when she heard and said they'd be down soon as they could. Terry gave her the hospital details. He said he could meet them if they wanted, by which time Jim's mum had already put the phone down. It was one of the longest journeys of Terry's life. He thought about everything and felt a massive sense of guilt about everything. The entire situation raged through his head. He got off the train a few stops early from the one to his hotel to try and clear his head. The visions of Jim lying there, with that tube sticking out of his mouth and the drips being fed into him, and all the shit he'd been through with Katrina, were constant thoughts.

Stopping at a pub, Terry got his drink and located a seat away from everybody in there.

He just needed to be alone. He wanted all this shit to be gone and to get Jim back to his music; it was what he needed. Terry was still in the pub when he received a call from Jim's folks letting him know they were heading down on the train and would be going straight to the hospital Terry stayed on for a few more drinks, then went to the toilets and splashed water on his face; he needed to get himself together for the journey back down to the hospital, l. Jim's parents were waiting in the reception, talking to a nurse when Terry arrived. Jim's mum went straight up to Terry and completely lost it.

"What the fuck was he doing getting involved with drugs? You were supposed to look out for him! We trusted you, and now he's up there dying from taking that shit. I suggest you get out of my fucking sight right now, before I do something I'll regret!"

Terry just sat down and held his head in his hands while he was getting this tirade from Jim's mum. Jim's dad pulled her away, explaining to her it wasn't Terry's fault and that Jim had a mind of his own. He then apologised to Terry, but that didn't make him feel any better.

The nurse had informed them of the toxicology report results, which came back as Jim having, alcohol, cannabis, cocaine and heroin in his system. Terry was lost for words. He thought to himself, "If he dies, it will be my fault. I'm the one who got him down here."

He left the hospital with all those thoughts cascading through his mind. He couldn't cope with it all.

Again he went to a few bars, trying to drink away all those thoughts of what was going on, but the more he drank the more he slid into the darkness of guilt.

When Will finally got back to the flat, he found Charlie asleep on the sofa and found Tom asleep in bed. He saw the state of the flat. He couldn't be doing with all this shit on top of everything else, so made his way down to the studio. He wanted to hear all the stuff they had done, but mainly to hear Jim's voice because he thought, "This could be the last time I ever hear him again."

Quinney was there at the studio. "All right, Will, how's things?"

"Hello, mate, could be better. I take it you've not heard about Jim?"

"No; what's happened? Everything okay?" Quinney asked.

"Not really. Jim's in hospital – suspected drug overdose. Err, would it be okay to listen to the songs again?"

Quinney was stunned by what he had just heard. "Yes, course you can. I'll just set it up for you. I hope he's okay."

When all was ready, Quinney clicked play on the console and out of all the songs to come first was the one about Ben. The tears started streaming down Will's face. He lit a cigarette, as Quinn had gone out. He took extra-long drags on it to try and calm his nerves. He slid out a bottle of vodka he had taken from the house. He didn't want to feel normal any more, or anything, for that matter. Just like everyone else, all this had taken a massive toll on Will and there was only one person to blame – Katrina. She could blame Jim for what he had done, but she knew what she was getting into with him. Will wanted a scapegoat; it was easy to blame her. He knew Jim could be a handful, but this was his best mate, plus he was the one lying in the hospital. She had fucked with his mind.

At the hospital, Jim's folks found him. By now he was sitting up having a cup of tea. Obviously he still wasn't feeling great and was sheet-white, like all the blood had been drained out of his body.

His mum sat next to him in floods of tears. "Why, Jim? Why?"

Jim shrugged. "Who knows why?" he said. The weakness in voice was telling that he didn't want to go through the whole scenario with them, as they would just go on. His dad sat there shaking his head.

"I thought something like this would happen. I mean, look at the people you go about with, the music you listen to," he said, not really helping the situation.

There was an uncomfortable silence. Jim's mum was staring into space, lost in her own little world. His dad just sat stoned-faced, shaking his head and huffing, just to let everyone know his take on this. Then the nurse came back in, asking if they would like any drinks, which broke the tension for a short time.

"Well," Jim said, "is this it? Have you come all the way down here just to have a go? If so then you can just leave. I can't be doing with any more negativity. I've had more than my fair share."

Jim's mum gave him a hug, which again didn't sit right with him because it never happened.

Before, except when Ben died, and even then it felt forced. It didn't feel natural to have any sort of affection from his parents. It had never happened as a kid and so he didn't see why it had to start now, and he didn't want any pity. He just wanted everyone to leave him alone. So Jim lay there in silence, staring at the ceiling, as if to give the hint to his folks that he was done. They stayed for a little while longer before leaving. They had brought some more clothes for him, and they put them in the side cupboard next to his bed. He nodded in appreciation, since he didn't have any more clothes with him, except at the flat.

He then turned away.

Chapter 30

Charlie was awoken by his phone ringing. It was the police, asking him if he knew a Terry Madelin. He sat up, clearing his throat, getting his head together.

"Hello, yeah, I know Terry. Anything wrong?"

"Well, a body was discovered down by the Hyde Park boating lake. A wallet was also found with his driver's licence, his phone and a notebook with numbers and addresses (Terry was old school, he still kept a book of numbers and addresses). Your number was at the top of that list. Would you be able to come down to St Mary's Hospital for identification?"

Charlie was stunned. "What – he's dead?"

He knew the answer but wanted it clarifying.

"I'm afraid so, sir, but we'd like for you to come to the hospital for an official identification."

"Okay, give me an hour." Charlie said.

"For fuck's sake – what else?" Charlie said while lighting a cigarette. He soon regretted thinking that, but he couldn't wrap his head around everything that was going on, what with Jim and his problems and now this.

Back at the studio, Will had finished listening to all the songs. He felt a lot better now, so he made his way back to the flat to get Tom, who he hoped was sober by now, even though that couldn't be guaranteed; he knew Tom had drunk a load of beer and a bottle of vodka. Tom was now awake, and he made his way downstairs. His head was banging from all the booze. He saw Charlie heading for the door. "Hey, where you going?" Tom said.

He saw the look on Charlie's face, his eyes all red. "Err just gotta nip out – back soon," Charlie said and slammed the door behind him.

"Oh, see yer then," Tom said while heading towards the kitchen, desperately in search of some painkillers, as his head was pounding. Katrina made her way through her front door, where she had found in her mail a letter from the landlord for late payments, since she had obviously neglected to pay any rent. She went and called on her ex for a shoulder to cry on, but he was far from in the mood for dishing out any sympathy.

"Oh right, so you've been down there, he knows the truth and he's fucked you off, am I right?" Joe said

"Yes, you're right. I thought we could make it work again, be good, like it was before."

"Make it work again? What, with me or him?" he said.

"You, always you," she said, trying to put on her most convincing self-pitying voice.

"Are you winding me up? It all went tits up down there and now suddenly you want me back. Well, you can do one. I'm not being used like that. I suggest you go back to Oxford and let your folks deal with it; plus, it wasn't any good before."

Katrina was left stunned by his abrupt, aggressive tone.

"But what about the baby? It is yours, you know!" Her voice too was suddenly taking on an aggressive tone. "My parents kicked me out. I'm not wanted back there."

"Ha! Seems like your folks know you as well" he quipped.

"You bastard!" she shouted.

"Oh yeah, and so what if it's mine? I don't want anything to do with it. You tried to pass it off as his, and now suddenly it's gone wrong and you want me back. It ain't gonna happen," Joe said, turning back to what he was doing.

"Are you really gonna turn me and your child away?" Katrina said.

Joe looked back round, his eyebrows furrowed.

"Don't you dare try and lay that guilt trip on me."

Katrina just stood there, like the world had just collapsed beneath her.

"Now shut the door on the way out, and don't come back," Joe said.

By now he had had more than enough of Katrina's mind games. That was it; she had nothing now. All the lies had caught up with her. She made her way back to her flat, went to the bathroom and took out a few boxes of different pills. She took a bottle of bourbon from the kitchen cupboard and cracked it open. As she slid down the wall, she lit up a cigarette, tears streaming down her face. "What have I done? What the fuck have I done?"

Chapter 31

Will got back to the flat quite the worse for wear. He found Tom in the living room playing on some computer game. Tom looked round and laughed at Will, who was staggering round, bumping into the walls.

"Well, look at the state of you," Tom joked. "I've only just sobered up and now you're steaming."

Will fell back into the one of the chairs. "Just been down the studio listening to some of the material. I had to just in case, you know, he doesn't make it."

Tom paused the game he was playing. "Is he really that bad?" he said, his face etched with a look of panic. He now really felt bad about not going down to see Jim.

"Right. I'll get you some strong coffee, and then I'll get going down there."

Tom's words were now forceful with a sense of urgency. When he returned, Will was out of it, snoring away. Tom got a blanket and covered him up. That whole conversation with Will rang round Tom's head, because if what Will said was true, this could be his last time he would see Jim. He needed to get down there. Tom grabbed Jim's acoustic, thinking it would bring him round. When he arrived at the hospital, he was quite nervous about seeing Jim, with what Will had told him. He lit a cigarette to try and calm himself, as he was still in the grips of a huge hangover. The alcohol sweats were very apparent when he entered the hospital, and the smell of the hospital overwhelmed him. He made a sharp dash to the toilet where he offloaded all his breakfast.

Tom then washed his face and composed himself the best he could before collaring a nurse. He asked her whereabouts Jim was staying. Will, in the state he was in, had completely forgotten that minor detail. He made his way up to the ward, buzzed in, and a ward nurse directed Tom to Jim's room and told him to be really quiet, as Jim still might be sleeping.

Tom knocked on the door. "Hello, mate, how's –"

He stopped mid-greeting when he found Jim's room empty. He called on the nurse to let her know that he wasn't in his room.

"Well, he should be in his room. I didn't see him leave; he may be in the TV room," the nurse said.

Tom got a bit wary. He went down to the TV room. Jim wasn't there.

"Well, he's not in that TV room," Tom said.

He then went to check if Jim was in the toilet. He soon discovered he wasn't. Tom went back to Jim's room and checked his wardrobe and the drawers. All were empty.

"Excuse me, you don't need to look any more. He's done a runner."

The panic on the nurse's face gave her a greyish complexion. Tom thought she was going to faint.

"Any ideas where he might be?" Tom questioned.

A senior nurse then came by asking what the situation was. She was then informed about the patient discharging himself.

Tom stood there, shaking. "Fucking disgrace."

The nurse came back with a blunt reply. "Well, if he doesn't want to be here then he has the right to leave at any time."

Tom looked at this nurse with complete disdain. "So you're telling me he can just leave? He may fucking die, and you don't give a shit!"

The nurse explained there was nothing they could do, and that Jim had made the decision to put himself in that situation. Tom left the ward, again shaking his head.

"Un-fucking-believable!"

He then tried calling Jim's phone, which was switched off.

Chapter 32

When Charlie arrived at the hospital, Tom was walking out one side. Charlie was coming in the other. Jim just happened to be in the same hospital where his friend and boss was lying on a cold slab. There were a couple of police officers waiting for him. While taking him down, they told him about the state he was in and to prepare himself. As they entered the cold-looking room, Charlie saw the figure of his friend laid out, a light-blue sheet covering him up. Charlie never got used to the smell of hospitals. They always unnerved him, but this place unnerved him a whole lot more, and with good reason. He moved slowly towards the trolley. The mortician stood on the other side of the trolley.

"Are you ready, sir?" he asked.

Charlie was now sweating profusely, readying himself for the sight that would befall him. He then slowly nodded. The mortician then removed part of the sheet. Charlie had his eyes shut, thinking of the nightmare reality about to unfold before him. He slowly opened them, and there he was. Terry had sustained substantial bruising to his head, his right eye bulged out from severe trauma, his nose was caved in, and he had swollen lips. Charlie turned away. He felt his stomach entering his mouth. He ran over to the sink and threw up all the contents of his last meal. He then ran the tap to let the cool water run over his head, feeling extremely dizzy. He sat down on the nearest chair.

"Are you okay there, sir?" one of the officers asked.

"Not really. It's not every day you see your mate lying on a slab with head his caved in." Charlie gathered himself, went back over and again looked at Terry.

"Well, so long mate. I will see you soon on the other side." He ran his hand over Terry's face. The freezing skin sent a chill all over his body.

The officers then took Charlie out to answer some routine questions, and he obliged. When all was done and signed, he was free to go. Charlie then rang round to let people close to Terry know the situation. He contacted Will about it, who said he couldn't get through to Jim to let him know what was happening.

"I've tried to call him but it keeps going to answer phone, but then again, with all the shit he's been through I suppose it wouldn't help him in anyway."

Will replied, "What! Terry's dead? Err, how? When?"

Charlie said he didn't know the full details, just that he'd been down to the hospital mortuary to identify Terry's body. The news of Terry's death totally sideswiped Will.

Will then said, "Well, to be honest, we'll never know for sure what he would think. He's done a runner from the hospital, and this whole thing is turning into a fucking nightmare."

Charlie was in full agreement. "Yep, I know what you're saying. Katrina's gone as well."

Will said bluntly, "Oh, fuck her. She is why Jim's in this mess. He couldn't handle the truth of that dirty slag!"

"Right, I better be off. I've got a band playing tonight, so take it easy and I hope you find Jim soon," Charlie said abruptly.

Before Will could ask if Charlie was going to help look for Jim, he rang off.

Will lit a cigarette. "What an absolute wanker," he thought, taking deep drags. Will's phone then went off. It was Tom.

"So, how is he?" Will said, his voice still quite weary like he'd just woken up.

"Well, Jim's done a runner" Tom said, Will then informed Tom of Terry's death and how Charlie's just basically said good luck and goodbye. Apparently he had more pressing issues with going to see another band he's promoting."

Tom said, "Hey, man, hold up. There's only so much info I can take at one time."

Tom was sitting outside the hospital, he told Will he had Jims guitar and what a waste of time it was him coming down, because he had discharged himself and was missing again. Before he then cottoned on to what Will had said.

"You say Terry's dead?" Tom said. He also couldn't believe this whole situation.

"For fuck's sake, Jim, not again," Will said. "So how did Terry die?" Tom questioned after.

"I'm not sure. Charlie didn't go into too much detail. He just told me he was trying to contact Jim and by the way, Terry's dead, and then, see yer later."

"Where are you now? I'll meet you." Will said.

"Still at the hospital. I'll wait here." Tom replied.

Will arrived at the hospital within the hour. They needed to go look for Jim again.

"He's really making a habit of this disappearing thing," Will said.

They both knew it was a needle in a haystack situation, but again they trolled the bars and talked to the people who looked the unsavoury types, for they knew he could be possibly be again looking for drugs. But, dead end after dead end. After searching for a good couple of hours, they decided to call it a night, heading back to the flat tired and deflated due to the fruitless search. They got back to the flat to find it was in complete darkness.

"For fuck's sake, Will, you didn't think to leave any lights on?" Tom said, obviously annoyed by Will's lack of forward thinking.

"Well, I didn't know what time we'd be back or if we were even getting back here tonight," Will said in his defence. "Anyway, I didn't want to use up any unnecessary electric, wasting it and that, costing money," Will said as an afterthought.

Tom just stared at him, his brow furrowed.

"Who cares about wasting the electricity? We're not paying for it, are we, you tit. Anyway, it's Charlie's place, so fuck him, I want to run up as much of a bill as I can after the way he treated me," Will said, obviously still pissed off from that last phone call he had had with Charlie. Tom shrugged as they went inside. There was a strong smell of weed floating round the downstairs.

"Did you leave a spliff on when you left?" Tom asked.

"Nope," came the instant reply.

"Then someone's here," Tom whispered.

Tom put Jims guitar down, went into the kitchen and pulled a big kitchen knife from the drawer.

"Now what are you gonna do with that?" Will scoffed.

"Well, if anybody comes out, I'm gonna fucking stick em," Tom said, making a stabbing motion.

Will just shook his head. "Fuck's sake."

They headed into the front room and switched on the lights. There was no one there. Then they moved into the hallway and heard a tapping coming from the living room, like someone was hitting their fingers on a table. Will pointed towards the living room door.

"Right, after three," he said, his hand on the door handle.

"One, two and three."

They burst in, screaming as loudly as they could and flicked the lights on. And who was sitting there at the dining table, calm as anything?

"Hello, boys," Jim said, flicking the ash from his spliff.

Will and Tom looked shocked.

"Where the fuck have you been!" Will shouted at Jim.

"I decided I was well enough to check myself out, so I did," Jim said with a starry-eyed smile. Tom flopped down on the sofa, placing the knife on the arm.

"We've been looking all round for you." Will said

"Sorry," Jim quipped. "Anyway, what were you gonna do with that knife?" Jim said. "Apparently he was gonna stick whoever it was in here," joked Will.

"Fucking hell, Tom, you haven't got it in you to do that. I know you too well," Jim said. Will and Tom proceeded to inform Jim of everything that had happened. Jim leant forward after hearing the news of Terry. He couldn't believe it. He dragged hard on his spliff.

"Do they know how it happened?" Jim said, feeling himself sink into that raging darkness. Jim started tearing up. He went over to the fridge, pulled a beer out and drank about half of it in one go, then he slumped back down into his seat and lit up a cigarette. The mood sank to a new low for Jim. That familiar dark hood enveloped him once again, his thoughts again testing his sanity, which was again on a knife's edge.

"No. I just got a call from Charlie and he told us Terry was gone. I think the police are investigating it," Will said.

Just then the door went and Charlie rolled in. "Hello, lads, how's it going?" Will and Tom just stared blankly at him.

"Cheers for leaving us in the lurch," Will said, very pissed off with him.

Charlie then saw Jim. "All right, Jim; where did you get to?"

Jim was silent for a minute and then said, "Oh, you know, I just wanted to go out and about. That hospital wasn't doing me any more favours, so I wanted out."

"Well, you're looking better," Charlie said with an uncomfortable smile.

Charlie then apologised. "I'm so sorry for not coming with you, but I had to get to that gig. It was a band I'm promoting. You understand, don't you, lads?" he said, looking at Will.

Jim flipped. "Oh, right, some fucking friend you are. Your so-called best mate is lying on a cold slab, and you fuck off to a gig."

Charlie again tried to apologise but Jim wasn't having any of it.

"All right, lads, let's pack up and move somewhere else!" Jim said.

Tom then tried to defuse the whole situation. "Look, guys, there's nothing we can do now, so how about we just sleep on it and talk again tomorrow?"

They all agreed. Charlie offered to buy them a takeout, as a sort of peace offering. They all opted for an Indian and a re-stock of beer. Charlie didn't argue and went out and got everything they wanted. Next morning Jim awoke on one of the couches, his head still buzzing from the previous night. They had eaten the food and demolished all the beer and a whole array of spirits and a ton of weed. Jim reached over and grabbed a book from his bag that he was reading; it was *Big Sur*, the alcohol-driven novel by Jack Kerouac. Jim started getting some ideas for music as he read, and he reached over for his guitar. He played a few chords, humming a tune to fit in with the melody. He was feeling it now. This is what it was all about, not the partying, the girls, etcetera. The music, the music was everything he needed. It was the one thing that drove him on, that took all his pains away. It cleansed his traumatised soul. It would never lie or cheat on him. It would never let him down, and that was that. Jim thought about everything that had happened.

"I don't need that shit any more; I don't need those ghosts in my mind. I'm done."

Jim had got his life more or less back on track with regular medication, and he wrote every day.

Jim, Will and Tom all managed to stay in London under the watchful eye of Charlie.

Terry was buried in the same cemetery as Ben, which they all attended. Back at the flat, Jim shouted upstairs, "Right, get your fucking arses down here; I've got a new tune."

Ben's song

A minor

First verse

We were only young, when we felt so strong

Would take on anyone we see

C, D, A minor

The trouble in our minds, when we didn't understand

But the fun we had, lent a helping hand

Chorus

G
But now you fly so high, taken too young to die D
I long for the time, we will meet again
C, G, A minor
So then until the end, when we meet again my friend
We'll remember you, just the way you were
Break D, C, A

Second verse

When I played you my songs, you would laugh then sing along

Would have your fun, and then be a helping hand

Hope you can see us now, has taken its toll with you not around

Still trying to move along, somehow

Chorus

But now you fly so high, taken too young to die

I long for the time, we will meet again

So then, until the end, when we meet again, my friend,

We'll remember you, just the way you were.

Ending break D, C, A

Rate this book on our website!

www.novum-publishing.co.uk

The author

Ian Lovell was born in 1973 in Leicester, where he attended South Wigston High School. He now lives in Leicestershire with his partner and has two children, Caitlin and Darcy. When not working for Royal Mail, Ian's passions are writing song lyrics, poetry and stories and playing the guitar and the harmonica. Ian started writing in the early nineties, while at the same time playing in a band, which has released three solo albums and a single. Ian has two published works – Realm of Reality, Rhyme and Dream and Life Through Light and Shadows.

novum 📖 PUBLISHER FOR NEW AUTHORS

The publisher

> *He who stops getting better stops being good.*

This is the motto of novum publishing, and our focus is on finding new manuscripts, publishing them and offering long-term support to the authors.
Our publishing house was founded in 1997, and since then it has become THE expert for new authors and has won numerous awards.

Our editorial team will peruse each manuscript within a few weeks free of charge and without obligation.

You will find more information about
novum publishing and our books on the internet:

w w w . n o v u m - p u b l i s h i n g . c o . u k

www.ingramcontent.com/pod-product-compliance
Ingram Content Group UK Ltd.
Pitfield, Milton Keynes, MK11 3LW, UK
UKHW040642060526
12295UKWH00010B/26